THE SCIENCE OF

HUMAN NATURE:

A PSYCHOLOGY FOR BEGINNERS

BY WILLIAM HENRY PYLE

CONTENTS

AUTHOR'S PREFACE

This book is written for young students in high schools and normal schools. No knowledge can be of more use to a young person than a knowledge of himself; no study can be more valuable to him than a study of himself. A study of the laws of human behavior,—that is the purpose of this book.

What is human nature like? Why do we act as we do? How can we make ourselves different? How can we make others different? How can we make ourselves more efficient? How can we make our lives more worth while? This book is a manual intended to help young people to obtain such knowledge of human nature as will enable them to answer these questions.

I have not attempted to write a complete text on psychology. There are already many such books, and good ones too. I have selected for treatment only such topics as young students can study with interest and profit. I have tried to keep in mind all the time the practical worth of the matters discussed, and the ability and experience of the intended readers.

TO THE TEACHER

This book can be only a guide to you. You are to help your students study human nature. You must, to some extent, be a psychologist yourself before you can teach psychology. You must yourself be a close and scientific student of human nature. Develop in the students the spirit of inquiry and investigation. Teach them to look to their own minds and their neighbor's actions for verification of the statements of the text. Let the students solve by observation and experiment the questions and problems raised in the text and the exercises. The exercises should prove to be the most valuable part of the book. The first two chapters are the most difficult but ought to be read before the rest of the book is studied. If you think best, merely read these two chapters with the pupils, and after the book is finished come back to them for careful study.

In the references, I have given parallel readings, for the most part to Titchener, Pillsbury, and Münsterberg. I have purposely limited the references, partly because a library will not be available to many who may use the book, and partly because the young student is likely to be confused by much reading from different sources before he has worked out some sort of system and a point of view of his own. Only the most capable members of a high school class will be able to profit much from the references given.

TO THE STUDENT

You are beginning the study of human nature. You can not study human nature from a book, you must study yourself and your neighbors. This book may help you to know what to look for and to understand what you find, but it can do little more than this. It is true, this text gives you many facts learned by psychologists, but you must verify the statements, or at least see their significance to *you*, or they will be of no worth to you. However, the facts considered here, properly understood and assimilated, ought to prove of great value to you. But perhaps of greater value will be the psychological frame of mind or attitude which you should acquire. The psychological attitude is that of seeking to find and understand the *causes of human action, and the causes, consequences, and significance of the processes of the human mind.* If your first course in psychology teaches you to look for these things, gives you some skill in finding them and in using the knowledge after you have it, your study should be quite worth while.

W. H. PYLE.

EDITOR'S PREFACE

There are at least two possible approaches to the study of psychology by teacher-training students in high schools and by beginning students in normal schools.

One of these is through methods of teaching and subject matter. The other aims to give the simple, concrete facts of psychology as the science of the mind. The former presupposes a close relationship between psychology and methods of teaching and assumes that psychology is studied chiefly as an aid to teaching. The latter is less complicated. The plan contemplates the teaching of the simple fundamentals at first and applying them incidentally as the occasion demands. This latter point of view is in the main the point of view taken in the text.

The author has taught the material of the text to high school students to the end that he might present the fundamental facts of psychology in simple form.

W. W. C.

CHAPTER I

INTRODUCTION

Science. Before attempting to define psychology, it will be helpful to make some inquiry into the nature of science in general. Science is knowledge; it is what we know. But mere knowledge is not science. For a bit of knowledge to become a part of science, its relation to other bits of knowledge must be found. In botany, for example, bits of knowledge about plants do not make a science of botany. To have a science of botany, we must not only know about leaves, roots, flowers, seeds, etc., but we must know the relations of these parts and of all the parts of a plant to one another. In other words, in science, we must not only *know*, we must not only have *knowledge*, but we must know the significance of the knowledge, must know its *meaning*. This is only another way of saying that we must have knowledge and know its relation to other knowledge.

A scientist is one who has learned to organize his knowledge. The main difference between a scientist and one who is not a scientist is that the scientist sees the significance of facts, while the non-scientific man sees facts as more or less unrelated things. As one comes to hunt for causes and inquire into the significance of things, one becomes a scientist. A thing or an event always points beyond itself to something else. This something else is what goes before it or comes after it,—is its cause or its effect. This causal relationship that exists between events enables a scientist to prophesy. By carefully determining what always precedes a certain event, a certain type of happening, a scientist is able to predict the event. All that is necessary to be able to predict an event is to have a clear knowledge of its true causes. Whenever, beyond any doubt, these causes are found to be present, the scientist knows the event will follow. Of course, all that he really *knows* is that such results have always followed similar causes in the past. But he has come to have faith in the uniformity and regularity of nature. The chemist does not find sulphur, or oxygen, or any other element acting one way one day under a certain set of conditions, and acting another way the next day under exactly the same conditions. Nor does the physicist find the laws of mechanics holding good one day and not the next.

The scientist, therefore, in his thinking brings order out of chaos in the world. If we do not know the causes and relations of things and events, the world seems a very mixed-up, chaotic place, where anything and everything is happening. But as we come to know causes and relations, the world turns out to be a very orderly and systematic place. It is a lawful world; it is not a world of chance. Everything is related to everything else.

Now, the non-scientific mind sees things as more or less unrelated. The far-reaching causal relations are only imperfectly seen by it, while the scientific mind not only sees things, but inquires into their causes and effects or consequences. The non-scientific man, walking over the top of a mountain and noticing a stone there, is likely to see in it only a stone and think nothing of how it came to be there; but the scientific man sees quite an interesting bit of history in the stone. He reads in the stone that millions of years ago the place where the rock now lies was under the sea. Many marine animals left their remains in the mud underneath the sea. The mud was afterward converted into rock. Later, the shrinking and warping earth-crust lifted the rock far above the level of the sea, and it may now be found at the top of the mountain. The one bit of rock tells its story to one who inquires into its causes. The scientific man, then, sees more significance, more meaning, in things and events than does the non-scientific man.

Each science has its own particular field. Zoölogy undertakes to answer every reasonable question about animals; botany, about plants; physics, about motion and forces; chemistry, about the composition of matter; astronomy, about the heavenly bodies, etc. The world has many aspects. Each science undertakes to describe and explain some particular aspect. To understand all the aspects of the world, we must study all the sciences.

A Scientific Law. By *law* a scientist has reference to uniformities which he notices in things and events. He does not mean that necessities are imposed upon things as civil law is imposed upon man. He means only that in certain well-defined situations certain events always take place, according to all previous observations. The Law of Falling Bodies may be cited as an example. By this law, the physicist means that in observing falling bodies in the past, he has noticed that they fall about sixteen feet in the first second and acquire in this time a velocity of thirty-two feet. He has noted that, taking into account the specific gravity of the object and the resistance of the air, this way of falling holds true of all objects at about the level of the sea.

The more we carefully study the events of the world, the more strongly we come to feel that definite causes, under the same circumstances, always produce precisely the same result. The scientist has faith that events will continue to happen during all the future in the same order of cause and effect in which they have been happening during all the past.

The astronomer, knowing the relations of the members of the solar system—the sun and planets—can successfully predict the occurrence of lunar and solar eclipses. In other fields, too, the scientist can predict with as much certainty as does the astronomer, provided his knowledge of the factors concerned is as complete as is the knowledge which the astronomer has of the solar system. Even in the case of human beings, uncertain as their actions seem to be, we can predict their actions when our knowledge of the factors is sufficiently complete. In a great many instances we do make such predictions. For example, if we call a person by name, we expect him to turn, or make some other movement in response. Our usual inability to make such predictions in the case of human beings is not because human beings are not subject to the law of cause and effect, it is not that their acts are due to chance, but that the factors involved are usually many, and it is difficult for us to find out all of them.

3

The Science of Psychology. Now, let us ask, what is the science of psychology? What kind of problems does it try to solve? What aspect of the world has it taken for its field of investigation?

We have said that each science undertakes to describe some particular aspect of the world. Human psychology is the science of human nature. But human nature has many aspects. To some extent, our bodies are the subject matter for physiology, anatomy, zoölogy, physics, and chemistry. Our bodies may be studied in the same way that a rock or a table might be studied. But a human being presents certain problems that a rock or table does not present. If we consider the differences between a human being and a table, we shall see at once the special field of psychology. If we stick a pin into a leg of the table, we get no response. If we stick a pin into a leg of a man, we get a characteristic response. The man moves, he cries out. This shows two very great differences between a man and a table. The man is *sensitive* and has the power of action, the power of *moving himself*. The table is not sensitive, nor can it move itself. If the pin is thrust into one's own leg, one has *pain*. Human beings, then, are sensitive, conscious, acting beings. And the study of sensitivity, action, and consciousness is the field of psychology. These three characteristics are not peculiar to man. Many, perhaps all, animals possess them. There is, therefore, an animal psychology as well as human psychology.

A study of the human body shows us that the body-surface and many parts within the body are filled with sensitive nerve-ends. These sensitive nerve-ends are the sense organs, and on them the substances and forces of the world are constantly acting. In the sense organs, the nerve-ends are so modified or changed as to be affected by some particular kind of force or substance. Vibrations of ether affect the eye. Vibrations of air affect the ear. Liquids and solutions affect the sense of taste. Certain substances affect the sense of smell. Certain organs in the skin are affected by low temperatures; others, by high temperatures; others, by mechanical pressure. Similarly, each sense organ in the body is affected by a definite kind of force or substance.

This affecting of a sense organ is known technically as *stimulation*, and that which affects the organ is known as the *stimulus*.

Two important consequences ordinarily follow the stimulation of a sense organ. One of these is movement. The purpose of stimulation is to bring about movement. To be alive is to respond to stimulation. When one ceases to respond to stimulation, he is dead. If we are to continue alive, we must constantly adjust ourselves to the forces of the world in which we live. Generally speaking, we may say that every nerve has one end in a sense organ and the other in a muscle. This arrangement of the nerves and muscles shows that man is essentially a sensitive-action machine. The problems connected with sensitivity and action and the relation of each to the other constitute a large part of the field of psychology.

We said just now, that a nerve begins in a sense organ and ends in a muscle. This statement represents the general scheme well enough, but leaves out an important detail. The nerve does not extend directly to a muscle, but ordinarily goes by way of the brain. The brain is merely a great group of nerve cells and fibers which have developed as a central organ where a stimulation may pass from almost any sense organ to almost any muscle.

But another importance attaches to the brain. When a sense organ is stimulated and this stimulation passes on to the brain and agitates a cell or group of cells there, *we are conscious*. Consciousness shifts and changes with every shift and change of the stimulation.

The brain has still another important characteristic. After it has been stimulated through sense organ and nerve, a similar brain activity can be revived later, and this revival is the basis of *memory*. When the brain is agitated through the medium of a sense organ, we have *sensation*; when this agitation is revived later, we have a *memory idea*. A study of consciousness, or mind, the conditions under which it arises, and all the other problems involved, give us the other part of the field of psychology.

We are not merely acting beings; we are *conscious* acting beings. Psychology must study human nature from both points of view. We must study man not only from the outside; that is, objectively, in the same way that we study a stone or a tree or a frog, but we must study him from the inside or subjectively. It is of importance to know not only how a man *acts*, but also how he *thinks and feels*.

It must be clear now, that human action, human behavior, is the main field of psychology. For, even though our main interests in people were in their minds, we could learn of the minds only through the actions. But our interests in other human beings are not in their minds but in *what they do*. It is true that our interest in ourselves is in our minds, and we can know these minds directly; but we cannot know directly the mind of another person, we can only guess what it is from the person's actions.

The Problems of Psychology. Let us now see, in some detail, what the various problems of psychology are. If we are to understand human nature, we must know something of man's past; we must therefore treat of the origin and development of the human race. The relation of one generation to that preceding and to the one following makes necessary a study of heredity. We must find out how our thoughts, feelings, sensations, and ideas are dependent upon a physical body and its organs. A study of human actions shows that some actions are unlearned while others are learned or acquired. The unlearned acts are known as *instincts* and the acquired acts are known as *habits*. Our psychology must, therefore, treat of instincts and habits.

How man gets experience, and retains and organizes this experience must be our problem in the chapters on sensations, ideas, memory, and thinking. Individual differences in human capacity make necessary a treatment of the different types and grades of intelligence, and the compilation of tests for determining these differences. We must also treat of the application of psychology to those fields where a knowledge of human nature is necessary.

6

Applied Psychology. At the beginning of a subject it is legitimate to inquire concerning the possibility of applying the principles studied to practical uses, and it is very proper to make this inquiry concerning psychology. Psychology, being the science of human nature, ought to be of use in all fields where one needs to know the causes of human action. And psychology is applicable in these fields to the extent that the psy chologist is able to work out the laws and principles of human action.

In education, for example, we wish to influence children, and we must go to psychology to learn about the nature of children and to find out how we can influence them. Psychology is therefore the basis of the science of education.

Since different kinds of work demand, in some cases, different kinds of ability, the psychology of individual differences can be of service in selecting people for special kinds of work. That is to say, we must have sometime, if we do not now, a psychology of professions and vocations. Psychological investigations of the reliability of human evidence make the science of service in the court room. The study of the laws of attention and interest give us the psychology of advertising. The study of suggestion and abnormal states make psychology of use in medicine. It may be said, therefore, that psychology, once abstract and unrelated to any practical interests, will become the most useful of all sciences, as it works out its problems and finds the laws of human behavior.

At present, the greatest service of psychology is to education. So true is this that a department has grown up called "educational psychology," which constitutes at the present time the most important subdivision of psychology. While in this book we treat briefly of the various applications of psychology, we shall have in mind chiefly its application to education.

The Science of Education. Owing to the importance which psychology has in the science of education, it will be well for us to make some inquiry into the nature of education. If the growth, development, and learning of children are all controlled and determined by definite causal factors, then a systematic statement of all these factors would constitute the science of education. In order to see clearly whether there is such a science, or whether there can be, let us inquire more definitely as to the kind of problems a science of education would be expected to solve.

There are four main questions which the science of education must solve: (1) What is the aim of education? (2) What is the nature of education? (3) What is the nature of the child? (4) What are the most economical methods of changing the child from what it is into what it ought to be?

The first question is a sociological question, and it is not difficult to find the answer. We have but to inquire what the people wish their children to become. There is a pretty general agreement, at least in the same community, that children should be trained in a way that will make them socially efficient. Parents generally wish their children to become honest, truthful, sympathetic, and industrious. It should be the aim of education to accomplish this social ideal. It should be the aim of the home and the school to subject children to such influences as will enable them to make a living when grown and to do their proper share of work for the community and state, working always for better things, and having a sympathetic attitude toward neighbors. Education should also do what it can to make people able to enjoy the world and life to the fullest and highest extent. Some such aim of education as this is held by all our people.

The second question is also answered. Psychological analysis reveals the fact that education is a process of becoming adjusted to the world. It is the process of acquiring the habits, knowledge, and ideals suited to the life we are to live. The child in being educated learns what the world is and how to act in it—how to act in all the various situations of life.

The third question—concerning the nature of the child—cannot be so briefly answered. In fact, it cannot be fully answered at the present time. We must know what the child's original nature is.

This means that we must know the instincts and all the other inherited capacities and tendencies. We must know the laws of building up habits and of acquiring knowledge, the laws of retention and the laws of attention. These problems constitute the subject matter of educational psychology, and at present can be only partially solved. We have, however, a very respectable body of knowledge in this field, though it is by no means complete.

The answer to the fourth question is in part dependent upon the progress in answering the third. Economical methods of training children must be dependent upon the nature of children. But in actual practice, we are trying to find out the best procedure of doing each single thing in school work; we are trying to find out by experimentation. The proper way to teach children to read, to spell, to write, etc., must be determined in each case by independent investigation, until our knowledge of the child becomes sufficient for us to infer from general laws of procedure what the procedure in a particular case should be. We venture to infer what ought to be done in some cases, but generally we feel insecure till we have proved our inference correct by trying out different methods and measuring the results.

Education will not be fully scientific till we have definite knowledge to guide us at every step. What should we teach? When should we teach it? How should we teach it? How poorly we answer these questions at the present time! How inefficient and uneconomical our schools, because we cannot fully answer them! But they are answerable. We can answer them in part now, and we know how to find out the answer in full. It is just a matter of patient and extensive investigation. We must say, then, that we have only the beginnings of a science of education. The problems which a science of education must solve are almost wholly psychological problems. They could not be solved till we had a science of psychology. Experimental psychology is but a half-century old; educational psychology, less than a quarter-century old. In the field of education, the science of psychology may expect to make its most important practical contribution. Let us, then, consider very briefly the problems of educational psychology.

Educational Psychology. Educational psychology is that division of psychology which undertakes to discover those aspects of human nature most closely related to education. These are (1) the original nature of the child—what it is and how it can be modified; (2) the problem of acquiring and organizing experience—habit-formation, memory, thinking, and the various factors related to these processes. There are many subordinate problems, such as the problem of individual differences and their bearing on the education of subnormal and supernormal children. Educational psychology is not, then, merely the application of psychology to education. It is a distinct science in itself, and its aim is the solving of those educational problems which for their solution depend upon a knowledge of the nature of the child.

The Method of Psychology. We have enumerated the various problems of psychology, now how are they solved? The method of psychology is the same as that of all other sciences; namely, the method of observation and experiment. We learn human nature by observing how human beings act in all the various circumstances of life. We learn about the human mind by observing our own mind. We learn that we *see* under certain objective conditions, *hear* under certain objective conditions, *taste, smell,feel cold* and *warm* under certain objective conditions. In the case of ourselves, we can know both our *actions* and our *mind*. In the case of others, we can know only their *actions*, and must infer their mental states from our own in similar circumstances. With certain restrictions and precautions this inference is legitimate.

We said the method of psychology is that of observation and experiment. The experiment is observation still, but observation subjected to exact methodical procedure. In a psychological experiment we set out to provide the necessary conditions, eliminating some and supplying others according to our object. The experiment has certain advantages. It enables us to isolate the phenomena to be studied, it enables us to vary the circumstances and conditions to suit our purposes, it enables us to repeat the observation as often as we like, and it enables us to measure exactly the factors of the phenomena studied.

A Psychological Experiment. Let us illustrate psychological method by a typical experiment. Suppose we wish to measure the individual differences among the members of a class with respect to a certain ability; namely, the muscular speed of the right hand. Psychological laboratories have delicate apparatus for making such a study. But let us see how we can do it, roughly at least, without any apparatus. Let each member of the class take a sheet of paper and a pencil, and make as many strokes as possible in a half-minute, as shown in Figure I. The instructor can keep the time with a stop watch, or less accurately with the second hand of an ordinary watch. Before beginning the experiment, the instructor should have each student taking the test try it for a second or two. This is to make sure that all understand what they are to do. When the instructor is sure that all understand, he should have the students hold their pencils in readiness above the paper, and at the signal, "Begin," all should start at the same time and make as many marks as possible in the half-minute. The strokes can then be counted and the individual scores recorded. The experiment should be repeated several times, say six or eight, and the average score for each individual recorded.

FIGURE I.—STROKES MADE IN THIRTY SECONDS.

A test of muscular speed

Whether the result in such a performance as this varies from day to day, and is accidental, or whether it is constant and fundamental, can be determined by repeating the experiment from day to day. This repetition will also show whether improvement comes from practice.

If it is decided to repeat the experiment in order to study these factors, constancy and the effects of practice, some method of studying and interpreting the results must be found. Elaborate methods of doing this are known to psychologists, but the beginner must use a simpler method. When the experiment is performed for the first time, the students can be ranked with reference to their abilities, the fastest one being called "first," the second highest, "second," and so on down to the slowest performer. Then after the experiment has been performed the second time, the students can be again ranked.

A rough comparison can then be made as follows: Determine how many who were in the best half in the first experiment are among the best half in the second experiment. If most who were among the best half the first time are among the best half in the second experiment, constancy in this performance is indicated. Or we might determine how many change their ranks and how much they change. Suppose there are thirty in the class and only four improve their ranks and these to the extent of only two places each. This would indicate a high degree of constancy. Two different performances can be compared as above described. The abilities on successive days can be determined by taking the average rank of the first day and comparing it with the average rank of the second day.

If the effects of practice are to be studied, the experiments must be kept up for many days, and each student's work on the first day compared with his work on succeeding days. Then a graph can be plotted to show the improvement from day to day. The average daily speed of the class can be taken and a graph made to show the improvement of the class as a whole. This might be plotted in black ink, then each individual student could put on his improvement in red ink, for comparison. A group of thirty may be considered as furnishing a fair average or norm in this kind of performance.

In connection with this simple performance, making marks as fast as possible, it is evident that many problems arise. It would take several months to solve anything like all of them. It might be interesting, for example, to determine whether one's speed in writing is related to this simple speed in marking. Each member of the class might submit a plan for making such a study.

The foregoing simple study illustrates the procedure of psychology in all experimentation. A psychological experiment is an attempt to find out the truth in regard to some aspect of human nature. In finding out this truth, we must throw about the experiment all possible safeguards. Every source of error must be discovered and eliminated. In the above experiment, for example, the work must be done at the same time of day, or else we must prove that doing it at different times of day makes no difference. Nothing must be taken for granted, and nothing must be assumed. Psychology, then, is like all the other sciences, in that its method of getting its facts is by observation and experiment.

SUMMARY. Science is systematic, related knowledge. Each science has a particular field which it attempts to explore and describe. The field of psychology is the study of sensitivity, action, and consciousness, or briefly, human behavior. Its main problems are development, heredity, instincts, habits, sensation, memory, thinking, and individual differences. Its method is observation and experiment, the same as in all other sciences.

CLASS EXERCISES

1.   Make out a list of things about human nature which you would like to know. Paste your list in the front of this book, and as you find your questions answered in this book, or in other books which you may read, check them off. At the end of the course, note how many remain unanswered. Find out whether those not answered can be answered at the present time.

2.   Does everything you do have a cause? What kind of cause?

3.   Human nature is shown in human action. Human action consists in muscular contraction. What makes a muscle contract?

4.   Plan an experiment the object of which shall be to learn something about yourself.

5.   Enumerate the professions and occupations in which a knowledge of some aspect of human nature would be valuable. State in what way it would be valuable.

6.   Make a list of facts concerning a child, which a teacher ought to know.

7.   Make a complete outline of Chapter I.

REFERENCES FOR CLASS READING

•   MÜNSTERBERG: *Psychology, General and Applied*, Chapters I, II, and V.

•   PILLSBURY: *Essentials of Psychology*, Chapter I.

•   PYLE: *The Outlines of Educational Psychology*, Chapter I.

•   TITCHENER: *A Beginner's Psychology*, Chapter I.

CHAPTER II

DEVELOPMENT OF THE RACE AND OF THE INDIVIDUAL

Racial Development. The purpose of this chapter is to make some inquiry concerning the origin of the race and of the individual. In doing this, it is necessary for us first of all to fix in our minds the idea of causality. According to the view of all modern science, everything has a cause. Nothing is uncaused. One event is the result of other previous events, and is in turn the cause of other events that follow. Yesterday flowed into to-day, and to-day flows into to-morrow. The world as it exists to-day is the result of the world as it existed yesterday. This is true not only of the inorganic world—the world of physics and chemistry—but it is true of living things as well. The animals and plants that exist to-day are the descendants of others that lived before. There is probably an unbroken line of descent from the first life that existed on the earth to the living forms of to-day.

Not only does the law of causality hold true in the case of our bodies, but of our minds as well. Our minds have doubtless developed from simpler minds just as our bodies have developed from simpler bodies. That different grades and types of minds are to be found among the various classes of animals now upon the earth, no one can doubt, for the different forms certainly show different degrees of mentality. According to the evidence of those scientists who have studied the remains of animals found in the earth's crust, there is a gradual development of animal forms shown in successive epochs. In the very oldest parts of the earth's crust, the remains of animal life found are very simple. In later formations, the remains show an animal life more complex. The highest forms of animals, the mammals, are found only in the more recent formations. The remains of man are found only in the latest formations.

15

Putting these two facts together—(1) that the higher types of mind are found to-day only in the higher types of animals, and (2) that a gradual development of animal forms is shown by the remains in the earth's crust—the conclusion is forced upon us that mind has passed through many stages of development from the appearance of life upon the earth to the present time. Among the lower forms of animals to-day one sees evidence of very simple minds. In amœbas, worms, insects, and fishes, mind is very simple. In birds, it is higher. In mammals, it is higher still. Among the highest mammals below man, we see manifestations of mind somewhat like our own. These grades of mentality shown in the animals of to-day represent the steps in the development of mind in the animals of the past.

We cannot here go into the proof of the doctrine of development. For this proof, the reader must be referred to zoölogy. One further point, however, may be noted. If it is difficult for the reader to conceive of the development of mind on the earth similar to the development of animals in the past, let him think of the development of mind in the individual. There can certainly be no doubt of the development of mind in an individual human being. The infant, when born, shows little manifestation of mentality; but as its body grows, its mind develops, becoming more and more complex as the individual grows to maturity.

The World as Dynamic. The view of the world outlined above, and held by all scientific men of the present time, may be termed the *dynamic* view. Man formerly looked upon the world as static, a world where everything was fixed and final. Each thing existed in itself and for itself, and in large measure independent of all other things. We now look upon things and events as related and dependent. Each thing is dependent upon others, related to others.

Man not only *lives in* such a world, but is *part of* such a world. In this world of constant and ceaseless change, man is most sensitive and responsive. Everything may affect him. To all of the constant changes about him he must adjust himself. He has been produced by this world, and to live in it he must meet its every condition and change. We must, then, look upon human nature as something coming out of the past and as being influenced every moment by the things and forces of the present. Man is not an independent being, unaffected by everything that happens; on the contrary, he is affected by all influences that act upon him. Among these influences may be mentioned weather, climate, food, and social forces.

The condition of the various organs of a child's body determine, to some extent, the effect which these various forces have upon it. If a child's eyes are in any way defective, making vision poor, this tremendously influences his life. Not only is such a child unable to see the world as it really is, but the eyestrain resulting from poor vision has serious effects on the child, producing all sorts of disorders. If a child cannot hear well or is entirely deaf, many serious consequences follow. In fact, every condition or characteristic of a child that is in any way abnormal may lead on to other conditions and characteristics, often of a serious nature. The growth of adenoids, for example, may lead to a serious impairment of the mind. Poor vision may affect the whole life and character of the individual. The influence of a parent, teacher, or friend may determine the interest of a child and affect his whole life. The correct view of child life is that the child is affected, in greater or less degree, by every influence which acts upon him.

Significance of Development and Causality. What are the consequences of the view just set forth? What is the significance of the facts that have been enumerated? It is of great consequence to our thinking when we come to recognize fully the idea of causality. We then fully accept the fact that man's body and mind are part of a causal and orderly world.

Let us consider, for example, the movement of a muscle. Every such movement must be caused. The physiologist has discovered what this cause is. Ordinarily and normally, a muscle contracts only when stimulated by a nerve current. Tiny nerve fibrils penetrate every muscle, ending in the muscle fibers. The nerve-impulse passing into the fibers of the muscles causes them to contract. The nerve stimulus itself has a cause; it ordinarily arises directly or indirectly from the stimulation of a sense organ. And the sense organs are stimulated by outside influences, as was explained previously.

Not only are our movements caused, but our sensations, our ideas, and our feelings follow upon or are dependent upon some definite bodily state or condition. The moment that we recognize this we see that our sensations, ideas, and feelings are subject to control. It is only because our minds are in a world of causality, and subject to its laws, that education is possible. We can bring causes to bear upon a child and change the child. It is possible to build up ideas, ideals, and habits. And ideas, ideals, and habits constitute the man. Training is possible only because a child is a being that can be influenced. What any child will be when grown depends upon what kind of child it was at the beginning and upon the influences that affect it during its early life while it is growing into maturity. We need have no doubt about the outcome of any particular child if we know, with some degree of completeness, the two sets of factors that determine his life—his inheritance and the forces that affect this inheritance. We can predict the future of a child to the extent that we know and understand the forces that will be effective in his life.

The notion of causality puts new meaning into our view of the *training* of a child. The doctrine of development puts new meaning into our notion of the *nature* of a child. We can understand man only when we view him genetically, that is, in the light of his origin. We can understand a child only in the light of what his ancestors have been.

As these lines are being written, the greatest, the bloodiest war of history is in progress. Men are killing men by thousands and hundreds of thousands. How can we explain such actions? Observation of children shows that they are selfish, envious, and quarrelsome. They will fight and steal until they are taught not to do such things. How can we understand this? There is no way of understanding such actions until we come to see that the children and men of to-day are such as they are because of their ancestors. It has been only a few generations, relatively speaking, since our ancestors were naked savages, killing their enemies and eating their enemies' bodies. The civilized life of our ancestors covers a period of only a few hundred years. The pre-civilized life of our ancestors goes back probably thousands and thousands of years. In the relatively short period of civilization, our real, original nature has been little changed, perhaps none at all. The modern man is, at heart, the same old man of the woods.

The improvements of civilization form what is called a social heritage, which must be impressed upon the original nature of each individual in order to have any effect. Every child has to learn to speak, to write, to dress, to eat with knife and fork; he must learn the various social customs, and to act morally as older people dictate. The child is by nature bad, in the sense that the nature which he inherits from the past fits him better for the original kind of life which man used to live than it does for the kind of life which we are trying to live now. This view makes us see that training a child is, in a very true sense, *making him over again*. The child must be trained to subdue and control his original impulses. Habits and ideals that will be suitable for life in civilized society *must be built up*. The doctrine of the Bible in regard to the original nature of man being sinful, and the necessity of regeneration, is fundamentally correct. But this regeneration is not so much a sudden process as it is the result of long and patient building-up of habits and ideals.

One should not despair of this view of child-life. Neither should one use it as an excuse for being bad, or for neglecting the training of children. On the contrary, taking the genetic view of childhood should give us certain advantages. It makes us see more clearly the *necessity* of training. Every child must be trained, or he will remain very much a savage. In the absence of training, all children are much alike, and all alike bad from our present point of view. The chief differences in children in politeness and manners generally, in morals, in industry, etc., are due, in the main, to differences in training. It is a great help merely to know how difficult the task of training is, and that training there must be if we are to have a civilized child. We must take thought and plan for the education and training of our children. The task of education is in part one of changing human nature. This is no light task. It is one that requires, in the case of each child, some twenty years of hard, patient, persistent work.

Individual Development. Heredity is a corollary of evolution. Individual development is intimately related to racial development. Indeed, racial development would be impossible without heredity in the individual. The individual must carry on and transmit what the race hands down to him. This will be evident when we explain what heredity means.

By heredity we mean the likeness between parent and offspring. This likeness is a matter of form and structure as well as likeness of action or response. Animals and plants are like the parents in form and structure, and to a certain extent their responses are alike when the individuals are placed in the same situation. A robin is like the parent robins in size, shape, and color. It also hops like the parent birds, sings as they do, feeds as they do, builds a similar nest, etc. But the likeness in action is dependent upon likeness in structure. The young robin acts as does the old robin, because the nervous mechanism is the same, and therefore a similar stimulus brings about a similar response.

Most of the scientific work in heredity has been done in the study of the transmission of physical characteristics. The main facts of heredity are evident to everybody, but not many people realize how far-reaching is the principle of resemblance between parent and offspring. From horses we raise horses. From cows we raise cows. The children of human beings are human. Not only is this true, but the offspring of horses are of the same stock as the parents. Not only are the colts of the same stock as the parents, but they resemble the parents in small details. This is also true of human beings. We expect a child to be not only of the same race as the parents, but to have family resemblances to the parents—the same color of hair, the same shape of head, the same kind of nose, the same color of eyes, and to have such resemblances as moles in the same places on the skin, etc. A very little investigation reveals likenesses between parent and offspring which we may not have expected before.

However, if we start out to hunt for facts of heredity, we shall perhaps be as much impressed by differences between parent and child as we shall by the resemblances. In the first place, every child has two parents, and it is often impossible to resemble both. One cannot, for example, be both short and tall; one cannot be both fair and dark; one cannot be both slender and heavy; one cannot have both brown eyes and blue. In some cases, the child resembles one parent and not the other. In other cases, the child looks somewhat like both parents but not exactly like either. If one parent is white and the other black, the child is neither as white as the one parent nor as black as the other.

The parents of a child are themselves different, but there are four grandparents, and each of them different from the others. There are eight great grandparents, and all of them different. If we go back only seven generations, covering a period of perhaps only a hundred and fifty years, we have one hundred and twenty-eight ancestors. If we go back ten generations, we have over a thousand ancestors in our line of descent. Each of these people was, in some measure, different from the others. Our inheritance comes from all of them and from each of them.

How do all of these diverse characteristics work out in the child? In the first place, it seems evident that we do not inherit our bodies as wholes, but in parts or units. We may think of the human race as a whole being made up of a great number of unit characters. No one person possesses all of them. Every person is lacking in some of them. His neighbor may be lacking in quite different ones. Now one parent transmits to the child a certain combination of unit characters; the other parent, a different combination. These characteristics may not all appear in the child, but all are transmitted through it to the next generation, and they are transmitted purely. By being transmitted purely, we mean that the characteristic does not seem to lose its identity and disappear in fusions or mixtures. The essential point in this doctrine of heredity is known as Mendelism; it is the principle of inheritance through the pure transmission of unit characters.

An illustration will probably make the Mendelian principle clear. Let us select our illustration from the plant world. It is found that if white and yellow corn are crossed, all the corn the first year, resulting from this crossing, will be yellow. Now, if this hybrid yellow corn is planted the second year, and freely cross-fertilized, it turns out that one fourth of it will be white and three fourths yellow. But this yellow consists of three parts: one part being pure yellow which will breed true, producing nothing but yellow; the other two parts transmit white and yellow in equal ratio. That is to say, these two parts are hybrids, the result of crossing white with yellow. It is not meant that one can actually distinguish these two kinds of yellow, the pure yellow and the hybrid yellow, but the results from planting it show that one third of the yellow is pure and that the other two thirds transmit white and yellow in equal ratio.

The main point to notice in all this is that when two individuals having diverse characteristics are crossed, the characteristics do not fuse and disappear ultimately, but that the two characteristics are transmitted in equal ratio, and each will appear in succeeding generations, and will appear pure, just as if it had not been crossed with something different. The first offspring resulting from the cross—known as hybrids—may show either one or the other of the diverse characteristics, or, when such a thing is possible, even a blending of the two characteristics. But whatever the actual appearance of the first generation of offspring resulting from crossing parents having diverse characteristics, their germ-cells transmit the diverse characteristics in equal proportion, as explained above.

When one of the diverse characteristics appears in the first generation of offspring and the other does not appear, or is not apparent, the one that appears is said to be *dominant*, while the one not appearing is said to be *recessive*. In our example of the yellow and white corn, yellow is dominant and white recessive. And it must be remembered that the white corn that appears in the second generation will breed true just as if it had never been crossed with the yellow corn. One third of the yellow of the second generation would also breed true if it could be separated from the other two thirds.

It is not here claimed that Mendelism is a universal principle, that all characteristics are transmitted in this way. However, the results of the numerous experiments in heredity lead one to expect this to be the case. Most of the experiments have been with lower animals and with plants, but recent experiments and statistical studies show that Mendelism is an important factor in human heredity, in such characteristics as color of hair and eyes and skin, partial color blindness, defects of eye, ear, and other important organs.

The studies that have been made of human heredity have been, for the most part, studies of the transmission of physical characteristics. Very little has been done that bears directly upon the transmission of mental characteristics. But our knowledge of the dependence of mind upon body should prepare us to infer mental heredity from physical heredity. Such studies as throw light on the question bear us out in making such an inference.

The studies that have been more directly concerned with mental heredity are those dealing with the resemblances of twins, studies of heredity in royalty, studies of the inheritance of genius, and studies of the transmission of mental defects and defects of sense organs. The results of all these studies indicate the inheritance of mental characteristics in the same way that physical characteristics are transmitted. Not only are human mental characteristics transmitted from parent to offspring, but they seem to be transmitted in Mendelian fashion.

Feeble-mindedness, for example, seems to be a Mendelian character and recessive. From the studies that have been made, it seems that two congenitally feeble-minded parents will have only feeble-minded children. Feeble-mindedness acts in heredity as does the white corn in the example given above. If one parent only is feeble-minded, the other being normal, all of the children will be normal, just as all of the corn, in the first generation after the crossing, was yellow. But these children whose parents are the one normal and the other feeble-minded, while themselves normal, transmit feeble-mindedness in equal ratio with normality. It works out as follows: If a feeble-minded person marry a person of sound mind and sound stock, the children will all be of sound, normal mind. If these children take as husbands and wives men and women who had for parents one normal and one feeble-minded person, their children will be one fourth feeble-minded and three fourths of them normal.

To summarize the various conditions: If a feeble-minded person marry a feeble-minded person, all the children will be feeble-minded. If a feeble-minded person marry a sound, normal person (pure stock), all the children will be normal. If the children, in the last case, marry others like themselves as to origin, one fourth of their offspring will be feeble-minded. If such hybrid children marry feeble-minded persons, one half of the offspring will be feeble-minded. It is rash to prophesy, but future studies of heredity may show that Mendelism, or some modification of the principle, always holds true of mind as well as of body.

Little can be said about the transmission of particular definite mental traits, such as the various aspects of memory, association, attention, temperament, etc. Before we can speak with any certainty here, we must make very careful experimental studies of these mental traits in parents and offspring. No such work has been done. All we have at the present time is the result of general observation.

Improvement of the Race. Eugenics is the science of improvement of the human race by breeding. While we can train children and thereby make them much better than they would be without such training, this training does not improve the stock. The improvement of the stock can be accomplished only through breeding from the best and preventing the poor stock from leaving offspring. This is a well-known principle in the breeding of domestic animals.

It is doubtless just as true in the case of human beings. The hygienic and scientific rearing of children is good for the children and makes their lives better, but probably does not affect their offspring. We should not forget that all the social and educational influences die with the generation that receives them. They must be impressed by training on the next generation or that generation will receive no influence from them. The characters which we acquire in our lifetime seem not to be transmitted to our children, except through what is known as social heredity, which is merely the taking on of characteristics through imitation. Our children must go through all the labor of learning to read, write, spell, add, multiply, subtract, and divide, which we went through. Moral traits, manners and customs, and other habits and ideals of social importance must be acquired by each successive generation.

Heredity *versus* Environment. The question is often asked whether heredity or the influence of environment has the most to do with the final outcome of one's life. It is a rather useless question to ask, for what a human being or anything else in the world does depends upon what it is itself and what the things and forces are that act upon it. Heredity sets a limitation for us, fixes the possibilities. The circumstances of life determine what we will do with our inherited abilities and characteristics. Hereditary influences incline us to be tall or short, fat or lean, light or dark. The characteristics of our memory, association, imagination, our learning capacity, etc., are determined by heredity. Of course, how far these various aspects develop is to some extent dependent upon the favorable or unfavorable influences of the environment. What is possible for us to do is settled by heredity; what we may actually do, what we may have the opportunity to do, is largely a matter of the circumstances of life.

In certain parts of New England, the number of men who become famous in art, science, or literature is very great compared to the number in some other parts of our country. As far as we have any

25

evidence, the native stocks are the same in the two cases, but in New England the influences turn men into the direction of science, art, and literature. Everything there is favorable. In other parts of the country, the influences turn men into other spheres of activity. They become large landowners, men of business and affairs.

The question may be asked whether genius makes its way to the front in spite of unfavorable circumstances. Sometimes it doubtless does. But pugnacity and perseverance are not necessarily connected with intellectual genius. Genius may be as likely to be timid as belligerent. Therefore unfavorable circumstances may crush many a genius.

The public schools ought to be on the watch for genius in any and all kinds of work. When a genius is found, proper training ought to be provided to develop this genius for the good of society as well as for the good of the individual himself. A few children show ability in drawing and painting, others in music, others in mechanical invention, some in literary construction. When it is found that this ability is undoubtedly a native gift and not a passing whim, special opportunity should be provided for its development and training. It will be better for the general welfare, as well as for individual happiness, if each does in life that for which he is by nature best fitted. For most of us, however, there is not much difference in our abilities. We can do one thing as well as we can many other things. But in a few there are undoubted special native gifts.

SUMMARY. This is an orderly world, in which everything has a cause. All events are connected in a chain of causes and effects. Human beings live in this world of natural law and are subject to it. Human life is completely within this world of law and order and is a part of it. Education is possible only because we can change human beings by having influences act upon them.

Individuals receive their original traits from their ancestors, probably as parts or units. Mendelism is the doctrine of the pure transmission of unit characters. Eugenics is the science of improving the human race by selective breeding. An individual's life is the result of the interaction of his hereditary characteristics and his environment.

CLASS EXERCISES

1.   Try to find rock containing the remains of animals. You can get information on such matters from a textbook on geology.

2.   Read in a geology about the different geological epochs in the history of the earth.

3.   Make a comparison of the length of infancy in the lower animals and in man. What is the significance of what you find? What advantage does it give man?

4.   What is natural selection? How does it lead to change in animals? Does natural selection still operate among human beings? (See a modern textbook on zoölogy.)

5.   By observation and from consulting a zoölogy, learn about the different classes of animal forms, from low forms to high forms.

6.   By studying domestic animals, see what you can learn about heredity. Enumerate all the points that you find bearing upon heredity.

7.   In a similar way, make a study of heredity in your family. Consider such characteristics as height, weight, shape of head, shape of nose, hair and eye color. Can you find any evidence of the inheritance of mental traits?

8.   Make a complete outline of Chapter II.

REFERENCES FOR CLASS READING

- DAVENPORT: *Heredity in Relation to Eugenics.*

- KELLICOTT: *The Social Direction of Human Evolution.*

CHAPTER III

MIND AND BODY

Gross Dependence. The relation of mind to body has always been an interesting one to man. This is partly because of the connection of the question with that of life after death. An old idea of this relation, almost universally held till recently, was that the mind or spirit lived in the body but was more or less independent of the body. The body has been looked upon as a hindrance to the mind or spirit. Science knows nothing about the existence of spirits apart from bodies. The belief that after death the mind lives on is a matter of faith and not of science. Whether one believes in an existence of the mind after death of the body, depends on one's religious faith. There is no scientific evidence one way or the other. The only mind that science knows anything about is bound up very closely with body. This is not saying that there is no existence of spirit apart from body, but that at present such existence is beyond the realm of science.

The dependence of mind upon body in a general way is evident to every one, upon the most general observation and thought. We know the effect on the mind of disease, of good health, of hunger, of fatigue, of overwork, of severe bodily injury, of blindness or deafness. We have, perhaps, seen some one struck upon the head by a club, or run over by an automobile, and have noted the tremendous consequences to the person's mind. In such cases it sometimes happens that, as far as we can see, there is no longer any mind in connection with that body. The most casual observation, then, shows that mind and body are in some way most intimately related.

Finer Dependence. Let us note this relation more in detail, and, in particular, see just which part of the body it is that is connected with the mind. First of all, we note the dependence of mind upon sense organs. We see only with our eyes. If we close the eyelids, we cannot see. If we are born blind, or if injury or disease destroys the retinas of the eyes or makes the eyes opaque so that light cannot pass through to the retinas, then we cannot see.

Similarly, we hear only by means of the ears. If we are born deaf, or if injury destroys some important part of the hearing mechanism, then we cannot hear. In like manner, we taste only by means of the taste organs in the mouth, and smell only with the organs of smell in the nose. In a word, our primary knowledge of the world comes only through the sense organs. We shall see presently just how this sensing or perceiving is accomplished.

Dependence of Mind on Nerves and Brain. We have seen how in a general way the mind is dependent on the body. We have seen how in a more intimate way it is dependent on the special sense organs. But the part of the body to which the mind is most directly and intimately related is the nervous system. The sense organs themselves are merely modifications of the nerve ends together with certain mechanisms for enabling stimuli to act on the nerve ends. The eye is merely the optic nerve spread out to form the retina and modified in certain ways to make it sensitive to ether vibrations. In addition to this, there is, of course, the focusing mechanism of the eye. So for all the sense organs; they are, each of them, some sort of modification of nerve-endings which makes them sensitive to some particular force or substance.

Let us make the matter clear by an illustration. Suppose I see a picture on the wall. My eyes are directed toward the picture. Light from the picture is refracted within the eyes, forming an image on each retina. The retina is sensitive to the light. The light produces chemical changes on the retina. These changes set up an excitation in the optic nerves, which is conducted to a certain place in the brain, causing an excitation in the brain. Now the important point is that when this excitation is going on in the brain, *we are conscious, we see the picture.*

As far as science can determine, we do not see, nor hear, nor taste, nor smell, nor have any other sensation unless a sense organ is excited and produces the excitation in the brain. There can be no doubt about our primary, sensory experience. By primary, sensory experience is meant our immediate, direct knowledge of any aspect of the world. In this field of our conscious life, we are entirely dependent upon sense organs and nerves and brain. Injuries to the eyes destroying their power to perform their ordinary work, or injuries to the optic nerve or to the visual center in the brain, make it impossible for us to see.

These facts are so self-evident that it seems useless to state them. One has but to hold his hands before his eyes to convince himself that the mind sees by means of eyes, which are physical sense organs. One has but to hold his hands tight over his ears to find out that he hears by means of ears—again, physical sense organs.

But simple and self-evident as the facts are, their acceptance must have tremendous consequences to our thinking, and to our view of human nature. If the mind is dependent in every feature on the body with its sense organs, this must give to this body and its sense organs an importance in our thought and scheme of things that they did not have before. This close dependence of mind upon body must give to the body a place in our scheme of education that it would not have under any other view of the mind. We wish to emphasize here that this statement of the close relation of the mind and body is not a theory which one may accept or not. It is a simple statement of fact. It is a presupposition of psychology. By "presupposition" is meant a fundamental principle which the psychologist always has in mind. It is axiomatic, and has the same place in psychology that axioms have in mathematics. All explanations of the working of the mind must be stated in terms of nerve and brain action, and stimulation of sense organs.

Since the sense organs are the primary and fundamental organs through which we get experience, and since the sensations are the elementary experiences out of which all mental life is built, it is necessary for us to have a clear idea of the sense organs, their structure and functions, and of the nature of sensations.

31

Vision. *The Visual Sense Organs*. The details of the anatomy of the eye can be looked up in a physiological textbook. The essential principles are very simple. The eye is made on the principle of a photographer's camera. The retina corresponds to the sensitive plate of the camera. The light coming from objects toward which the eyes are directed is focused on the retina, forming there an image of the object. The light thus focused on the retina sets up a chemical change in the delicate nerve tissue; this excitation is transmitted through the optic nerve to the occipital (back) part of the brain, and sets up brain action there. Then we have visual sensation; we see the object.

The different colors that we see are dependent upon the vibration frequency of the ether. The higher frequencies give us the colors blue and green, and the lower frequencies give us the colors yellow and red. The intermediate frequencies give us the intermediate colors blue-green and orange. By vibration frequencies is meant the rate at which the ether vibrates, the number of vibrations a second. If the reader wishes to know something about these frequencies, such information can be found in a textbook on physics.

It will be found that the vibration rates of the ether are very great. It is only within a certain range of vibration frequency that sunlight affects the retina. Slower rates of vibration than that producing red do not affect the eye, and faster than that producing violet do not affect the eye. The lightness and darkness of a color are dependent upon the intensity of the vibration. Red, for example, is produced by a certain vibration frequency. The more intense the vibration, the brighter the red; the less intense, the darker the red.

When all the vibration frequencies affect the eyes at the same time, we see no color at all but only brightness. This is due to the fact that certain vibration frequencies neutralize each other in their effect on the retina, so far as producing color is concerned. Red neutralizes green, blue neutralizes yellow, violet neutralizes yellowish green, orange neutralizes bluish green.

All variations in vision as far as color and brightness are concerned are due to variations in the stimulus. Changes in vibration frequency give the different colors. Changes in intensity give the different brightnesses: black, gray, and white. All explanations of the many interesting phenomena of vision are to be sought in the physiological action of the eye.

Besides the facts of color and light and shade, already mentioned, some further interesting visual phenomena may be mentioned here.

Visual Contrast. Every color makes objects near it take on the antagonistic or complementary color. Red makes objects near appear green, green makes them appear red. Blue makes near objects appear yellow, while yellow makes them appear blue. Orange induces greenish blue, and greenish blue induces orange. Violet induces yellowish green, and yellowish green induces violet. These color-pairs are known as antagonistic or complementary colors. Each one of a pair enhances the effect of its complementary when the two colors are brought close together. In a similar way, light and dark tints act as complementaries. Light objects make dark objects near appear darker, and dark objects make light objects near seem lighter.

These universal principles of contrast are of much practical significance. They must be taken account of in all arrangements of colors and tints, for example, in dress, in the arrangement of flowers and shrubs, in painting.

Color-Mixture. If, on a rotating motor, disks of different colors—say red and yellow—are placed and rotated, one sees on looking at them not red or yellow but orange. This phenomenon is known as *color-mixture*. The result is due to the simultaneous stimulation of the retina by two kinds of ether vibration. If the colors used are a certain red and a certain green, they neutralize each other and produce only gray. All the pairs of complementary colors mentioned above act in the same way, producing, if mixed in the right proportion, no color, but gray. If colored disks not complementary are mixed by rotation on a motor, they produce an intermediate

33

color. Red and yellow give orange. Blue and green give bluish green. Yellow and green give yellowish green. Red and blue give violet or purple, depending on the proportion. Mixing pigments gives, in general, the same results as mixing by means of rotating the disks. The ordinary blue and yellow pigments give green when mixed, because each of the two pigments contains green. The blue and yellow neutralize each other, leaving green.

Visual After-Images. The stimulation of the retina has interesting after effects. We shall mention here only the one known as *negative after-images.* If one will place on the table a sheet of white paper, and on this white paper lay a small piece of colored paper, and if he will then gaze steadily at the colored paper for a half-minute, it will be found that if the colored paper is removed one sees its complementary color. If the head is not moved, this complementary color has the same size and shape as the original colored piece of paper. The negative after-image can be projected on a background at different distances, its size depending on the distance of the background. The after-image will be found to mix with an objective color in accordance with the principles of color-mixture mentioned above.

After-image phenomena have some practical consequences. If one has been looking at a certain color for some time, a half-minute or more, then looks at some other color, the after-image of the first color mixes with the second color.

Adaptation. The fact last mentioned leads us to the subject of adaptation. If the eyes are stimulated by the same kind of light for some time, the eyes become adapted to that light. If the light is yellow, at first objects seem yellow, but after a time they look as if they were illuminated with white light, losing the yellow aspect. But if one then goes out into white light, everything looks bluish. The negative after-image of the yellow being cast upon everything makes the surroundings look blue, for the after-image of yellow is blue. All the other colors act in a similar way, as do also black and white. If one has been for some time in a dark room and then goes out to a lighter place, it seems unusually light. And if one goes from the light to a dark room, it seems unusually dark.

Hearing or Audition. Just as the eye is an organ sensitive to certain frequencies of ether vibration, so the ear is an organ sensitive to certain air vibrations. The reader should familiarize himself with the physiology of the ear by reference to physiologies. The drum-skin, the three little bones of the middle ear, and the cochlea of the inner ear are all merely mechanical means of making possible the stimulation of the specialized endings of the auditory nerve by vibrations of air.

As the different colors are due to different vibration frequencies of the ether, so different pitches of sound are due to differences in the rates of the air vibrations. The low bass notes are produced by the low vibration frequencies. The high notes are produced by the high vibration frequencies. The lowest notes that we can hear are produced by about twenty vibrations a second, and the highest by about forty thousand vibrations a second.

Other Sense Organs. We need not give a detailed statement of the facts concerning the other senses. In each case the sense organ is some special adaptation of the nerve-endings with appropriate apparatus in connection to enable it to be affected by some special thing or force in the environment.

In the case of taste, we find in the mouth, chiefly on the back and edges of the tongue, organs sensitive to sweet, sour, salt, and bitter. In the nose we have an organ that is sensitive to the tiny particles of substances that float in the air which we breathe in through the nose.

In the skin we find several kinds of sense organs that give us the sensations of cold and warmth, of pressure and pain. These are all special and definite sensations produced by different kinds of organs. The sense of warmth is produced by different organs from those which produce the sense of cold. These organs can be detected and localized on the skin. So, also, pain and touch or pressure have each its particular organ.

Within the body itself we have sense organs also, particularly in the joints and tendons and in the muscles. These give us the sensations which are the basis of our perception of motion, and of the position of the body and its members. In the semicircular canals of the inner ear are organs that give us the sense of dizziness, and enable us to maintain our equilibrium and to know up from down.

The general nature of the sense organs and of sensa tion should now be apparent. The nervous system reaches out its myriad fingers to every portion of the surface of the body, and within the body as well. These nerve-endings are specially adapted to receive each its particular form of stimulation. This stimulation of our sense organs is the basis or cause of our sensations. And our sensations are the elementary stuff of all our experience. Whatever thoughts we have, whatever ideas or images we have, they come originally from our sensations. They are built up out of our sensations or from these sensations as they exist in memory.

Defects of Sense Organs. The organs of sight and hearing are now by far the most important of our sense organs. They enable us to sense things that are at a distance. We shall therefore discuss defects of these two organs only. Since sensations are the primary stuff out of which mind is made, and since sight and hearing are the most important sense organs, it is evident that our lives are very much dependent on these organs. If they cannot do their work well, then we are handicapped. And this is often the case.

The making of the human eye is one of the most remarkable achievements of nature. But the making of a perfect eye is too big a task for nature. She never makes a perfect eye. There is always some defect, large or small. To take plastic material and make lenses and shutters and curtains is a great task. The curvature of the front of the eye and of the front and back of the crystalline lens is never quite perfect, but in the majority of cases it is nearly enough perfect to give us good vision. However, in about one third of school children the defect is great enough to need to be corrected by glasses.

The principle of the correction of sight by means of glasses is merely this. When the focusing apparatus of the eye is not perfect, it can be made so by putting in front of the eye the proper kind of lens. There is nothing strange or mysterious about it. In some cases, the eye focuses the light before it reaches the retina. Such cases are known as nearsightedness and are corrected by having placed in front of the eyes concave lenses of the proper strength. These lenses diverge the rays and make them focus on the retina. In other cases, the eye is not able to focus the rays by the time they reach the retina. In these cases, the eyes need the help of convex lenses of the proper strength to make the focus fall exactly on the retina.

The teacher should explain these principles and illustrate by drawings. Consult a good text in physiology. Noyes' University of Missouri Extension Bulletin on eye and ear defects will be found most useful.

Another defect of the eye, known as astigmatism, is due to the fact that the eye does not always have a perfectly spherical front (cornea). The curvature in one direction is different from that in others. For example, the vertical curvature may be more convex than the horizontal. Such a condition produces a serious defect of vision. It can be corrected by means of cylindrical lenses of the proper strength so placed before the eye as to correct the defect in curvature.

Still another defect of vision is known as presbyopia or farsightedness due to old age. It has the following explanation: In early life, when we look at near objects, the crystalline lens automatically becomes thicker, more convex. This adjustment brings the rays to a focus on the retina, which is required for good vision. As we get old, the crystalline lens loses its power to change its adjustment for near objects, al though the eye may see at a distance as well as ever. The old person, therefore, must wear convex glasses when looking at near objects, as in reading and sewing.

Another visual defect of a different nature is known as partial color blindness. The defects described above are due to misshapen eyes. Partial color blindness is due to a defect of the retina which makes it unable to be affected by light waves producing red and green. A person with this defect confuses red and green. While only a small percentage of the population has this defect, it is nevertheless very important that those having it be detected. People having the defect should not be allowed to enter occupations in which the seeing of red and green is important. It was recently brought to the author's attention that a partially color-blind man was selling stamps in a post office. Since two denominations of stamps are distinguished by red and green colors, this man made frequent mistakes. He was doing one of the things for which he was specially unfitted. It is easy to detect color blindness by simple tests.

So great is the importance of good vision in school work and the later work of life, that every teacher should know how to make simple tests to determine visual defects. Children showing any symptoms of eyestrain should be required to have their visual defects corrected by a competent oculist, and should be warned not to have the correction made by a quack. There is great popular ignorance and even prejudice concerning visual defects, and it is very important that teachers have a clear understanding of the facts.

Defects of Hearing. Hearing defects are only about half as frequent as those of sight. They are nearly all due to catarrhal infection of the middle ear through the Eustachian tube. The careful and frequent medical examination of school children cannot, therefore, be too strongly emphasized. The deafness or partial deafness that comes from this catarrhal infection can seldom be cured; it must be prevented by the early treatment of the troubles which cause it.

SUMMARY. The mind is closely related to the body. Especially is it dependent upon the brain, nerves, and sense organs. The sense organs are special adaptations of the nerve-ends for receiving impressions. Each sense organ receives only its particular type of impression.

The main visual phenomena are those of color-mixture, after-images, adaptation, and contrast. Since sensation is the basis of mental life, defects of the sense organs are serious handicaps and should be corrected if possible. Visual defects are usually due to a misshapen eyeball and can be corrected by proper glasses, which should be fitted by an oculist. Hearing defects usually arise from catarrhal trouble in the middle ear.

CLASS EXERCISES

1.   Make a study of the relation of the mind to the body. Enumerate the different lines of evidence which you may find indicating their close relationship.

2.   Can you find any evidence tending to show that the mind is independent of the body?

3.   *Color-Mixture.* Colored disks can be procured from C. H. Stoelting Company, Chicago. If a small motor is available, the disks can be rotated on the motor and the colors mixed. Mix pairs of complementary colors, also pairs of non-complementary colors, and note the result. A simple device can be made for mixing colors, as follows: On a board stand a pane of glass. On one side of the glass put a colored paper and on the other side of the glass put a different color. By looking through the glass you can see one color through transmitted light and the other color through reflected light. By inclining the glass at different angles you can get different proportions of the mixture, now more of one color, now more of the other.

4.   *Negative After-Images.* Cut out pieces of colored paper a half inch square. Put one of these on a white background on the table.

With elbows on the table, hold the head in the hands and gaze at the colored paper for about a half-minute, then blow the paper away and continue to gaze at the white background. Note the color that appears. Use different colors and tabulate the results. Try projecting the after-images at different distances. Project the after-images on different colored papers. Do the after-images mix with the colors of the papers?

5.   An interesting experiment with positive after-images can be performed as follows: Shut yourself in a dark closet for fifteen or twenty minutes to remove all trace of stimulation of the retina. With the eyes covered with several folds of thick black cloth go to a window, uncover the eyes and take a momentary look at the landscape, immediately covering the eyes again. The landscape will appear as a positive after-image, with the positive colors and lights and shades. The experiment is best performed on a bright day.

6.   *Adaptation.* Put on colored glasses or hold before the eyes a large piece of colored glass. Note that at first everything takes on the color of the glass. What change comes over objects after the glasses have been worn for fifteen or twenty minutes? Describe your experience after removing the glasses. Plan and perform other experiments showing adaptation. For illustration, go from a very bright room into a dark room. Go from a very dark room to a light one. Describe your experience.

7.   *Contrast.* Take a medium gray paper and lay it on white and various shades of gray and black paper. Describe and explain what you find.

8.   *Color Contrast.* Darken a room by covering all the windows except one window pane. Cover it with cardboard. In the cardboard cut two windows six inches long and one inch wide. Over one window put colored glass or any other colored material through which some light will pass. By holding up a pencil you can cast two shadows on a piece of paper. What color are the shadows? One is a contrast color induced by the other; which one? Explain the results.

9.   Make a study of the way in which women dress. What do you learn about color effects?

10.   From the Stoelting Company you can obtain the Holmgren worsteds for studying color blindness.

11.   *Defective Vision.* Procure a Snellen's test chart and determine the visual acuity of the members of the class. Seat the subject twenty feet from the chart, which should be placed in a good light. While testing one eye, cover the other with a piece of cardboard. Above each row of letters on the chart is a number which indicates the distance at which it can be read by a normal eye. If the subject can read only the thirty-foot line, his vision is said to be 20/30; if only the forty-foot line, the vision is 20/40. If the subject can read above the twenty-foot line and complains of headache from reading, farsightedness is indicated. If the subject cannot read up to the twenty-foot line, nearsightedness or astigmatism is indicated.

12.   *Hearing.* By consultation with the teacher of physics, plan an experiment to show that the pitch of tones depends on vibration frequency. Such an experiment can be very simply performed by rotating a wheel having spokes. Hold a light stick against the spokes so that it strikes each spoke. If the wheel is rotated so as to give twenty or thirty strokes a second, a very low tone will be heard. By rotating the wheel faster you get a higher tone. Other similar experiments can be performed.

13.   Acuity of hearing can be tested by finding the distance at which the various members of the class can hear a watch-tick. The teacher can plan an experiment using whispering instead of the watch-tick. (See the author's *Examination of School Children.*)

14.   By using the point of a nail, one can find the "cold spots" on the skin. Warm the nail to about 40 degrees Centigrade and you can find the "warm spots."

15.   By touching the hairs on the back of the hand, you can stimulate the "pressure spots."

16.   By pricking the skin with the point of a needle, you can stimulate the "pain spots."

17.   The sense of taste is sensitive only to solutions that are sweet, sour, salt, or bitter. Plan experiments to verify this point. What we call the "taste" of many things is due chiefly to odor. Therefore in experiments with taste, the nostrils should be stopped up with cotton. It will be found, for example, that quinine and coffee are indistinguishable if their odors be eliminated by stopping the nose. The student should compare the taste of many substances put into the mouth with the nostrils open with the taste of the same substances with the nostrils closed.

REFERENCES FOR CLASS READING

- COLVIN AND BAGLEY: *Human Behavior*, Chapters VII and XII.

- MÜNSTERBERG: *Psychology, General and Applied*, Chapters III, IV, VI, and VII.

- PILLSBURY: *Essentials of Psychology*, Chapters II, III, and IV.

- PYLE: *The Outlines of Educational Psychology*, Chapter II.

- TITCHENER: *A Beginner's Psychology*, Chapter I, par. 3; also Chapter II.

CHAPTER IV

INHERITED TENDENCIES

Stimulus and Response. We have learned something about the sense organs and their functions. We have seen that it is through the sense organs that the world affects us, stimulates us. And we have said that we are stimulated in order that we may respond.

We must now inquire into the nature of our responses. We are moving, active beings. But how do we move, how do we act when stimulated? Why do we do one thing rather than another? Why do we do one thing at one time and a different thing at another time?

Before we answer these questions it will be necessary for us to get a more definite and complete idea of the nature of stimulus and response. We have already used these terms, but we must now give a more definite account of them. It was said in the preceding chapter that when a muscle contracts, it must first receive a nerve-impulse. Now, anything which starts this nerve-impulse is called the stimulus. The muscular movement which follows is, of course, the response. The nervous system forms the connection between the stimulus and response.

The stimulus which brings about a response may be very simple. Or, on the other hand, it may be very complex. If one blows upon the eyelids of a baby, the lids automatically close. The blowing is the stimu lus and the closing of the lids is the response. Both stimulus and response are here very simple.

But sometimes the stimulus is more complex, not merely the simple excitation of one sense organ, but a complicated stimulation of an organ, or the simultaneous stimulation of several organs. In playing ball, the stimulus for the batter is the on-coming ball. The response is the stroke. This case is much more complex than the reflex closing of the eyelids. The ball may be pitched in many different ways and the response changes with these variations.

In piano playing, the stimulus is the notes written in their particular places on the staff. Not only must the position of the notes on the staff be taken into account, but also many other things, such as sharps and flats, and various characters which give directions as to the manner in which the music is to be played. The striking of the notes in the proper order, in the proper time, and with the proper force, is the response.

In typewriting, the stimulus is the copy, or the idea of what is to be written, and the response is the striking of the keys in the proper order. Speaking generally, we may say that the stimulus is the force or forces which excite the sense organs, and thereby, through the nervous system, bring about a muscular response.

This is the ordinary type of action, but we have already indicated a different type. In speaking of typewriting we said the stimulus might be either the copy or ideas. One can write from copy or dictation, in which the stimulus is the written or spoken word, but one can also write as one thinks of what one wishes to write. The latter is known as *centrally initiated action*. That is to say, the stimulus comes from within, in the brain, rather than from without.

Let us explain this kind of stimulation a little further. Suppose I am sitting in my chair reading. I finish a chapter and look at my watch. I notice that it is three o'clock, and recall that I was to meet a friend at that time. The stimulus in this case is in the brain itself; it is the nervous activity which corresponds to the idea of meeting my friend. If we disregard the distinction between mind and body, we may say that the stimulus for a response may be an idea as well as a perception, the perception arising from the immediate stimulation of a sense organ, and the idea arising from an excitation of the brain not caused by an immediate stimulation of a sense organ.

Instincts and Habits. In human action it is evident that there is always a stimulus to start the nerve-impulse which causes the action. If we make inquiry concerning the connection between the stimulus and response; if we ask how it has come about that a particular stimulus causes a particular response rather than some other possible response, we find two kinds of causes. In one case the causal connection is established through heredity; in the other, the causal connection is established during a person's lifetime through training.

A chicken, for example, hides under some cover the first time it hears the cry of a hawk; it scratches the first time its feet touch sand or gravel; it pecks the first time it sees an insect near by. An infant closes its eyes the first time it feels cold wind blow upon them; it cries the first time it feels pain; it clasps its fingers together the first time a touch is felt inside them. The child's nervous system is so organized that, in each of the cases named, the stimulus brings forth the particular, definite response. These acts do not have to be learned.

But it is quite different in typewriting and piano playing. One *must learn* what keys on the piano to strike in response to the various situations of the notes as written in the music. One must also learn the keys on the typewriter before he can operate a typewriter. And in the case of other habits, we find, for example, that one does not respond by saying "81" for 9 times 9; nor "13" for 6 plus 7; nor "8" for 15 minus 7; nor "8" for the square root of 64; nor "144" for the square of 12, etc., until one has learned in each case.

Some connections between stimulus and response we have through inheritance; all others are built up and established in one's lifetime, particularly in the first thirty years of one's life.

We have spoken of bonds between stimulus and response, but have not explained just what can be meant by a *bond.* In what sense are stimulus and response bound together? A bond is a matter of greater permeability, of less resistance in one direction through the nervous system than in other directions. Nerves are conductors for nerve-currents. When a nerve-current is started in a sense organ, it passes on through the path of least resistance.

Now, some nerves are so organized and connected through inheritance as to offer small resistance. This forms a ready-made connection between stimulus and response. Muscular responses that are connected with their stimuli through inherited bonds, by inherited nerve structure, are called instincts. Those that are connected by acquired bonds are called habits. Sucking, crying, laughing, are instinctive acts. Adding, typewriting, piano playing, are habits.

The term *instinct* may be given to the act depending upon inherited structure, an inherited bond, or it may be given to the inherited bond itself. Similarly, the term *habit* may be given to an act that we have had to learn or to the bond which we ourselves establish between response and stimulus. In this book we shall usually mean by instinct an action depending upon inherited structure and by habit an act depending upon a bond established during lifetime. A good part of our early lives is spent in building up bonds between stimuli and responses. This establishing of bonds or connections is called *learning*.

Appearance of Inherited Tendencies. Not all of our inherited tendencies are manifested immediately after birth, nor indeed in the earliest years of childhood, but appear at different stages of the child's growth. It has already been said that a child, soon after birth, will close its eyelids when they are blown upon. The lids do not close at this time if one strikes at them, but they will do this later. The proper working of an instinct or an inherited tendency, then, depends upon the child's having reached a certain state of development.

The maturing of an instinct depends upon both age and use, that is to say, upon the age of the animal and the amount of use or exercise that the instinctive activity has had. The most important factor, however, seems to be age. While our knowledge of the dependence of an instinct upon the age of the animal is not quite so definite in the case of human instincts, the matter has been worked out in the case of chickens.

The experiment was as follows: Chickens were taken at the time of hatching, and some allowed to peck from the first, while others were kept in a dark room and not allowed to peck. When the chickens were taken out of the dark room at the end of one, two, three, and four days, it was found that in a few hours they were peck ing as well as those that had been pecking from birth. It seems probable, if we may judge from our limited knowledge, that in the human child, activities are for the most part dependent upon the age of the child, and upon the state of development of the nervous system and of the organs of the body.

Significance of Inherited Tendencies. Although human nature is very complex, although human action nearly always has some element of habit in it, nevertheless, inborn tendencies are throughout life powerful factors in determining action. This will at once be apparent if we consider how greatly we are influenced by anger, jealousy, love, fear, and competition. Now we do not have to learn to be jealous, to hate, to love, to be envious, to fight, or to fear. These are emotions common to all members of the human race, and their expression is an inborn tendency. Throughout life no other influences are so powerful in determining our action as are these. So, although most of our detailed actions in life are habits which we learn or acquire, the fundamental influences which decide the course of our action are inherited tendencies.

Classification of Instincts. For convenience in treatment the instincts are grouped in classes. Those instincts most closely related to individual survival are called *individualistic* instincts. Those more closely related to the survival of the group are called *socialistic*. Those individualistic tendencies growing out of periodic changes of the environment may be called *environmental* instincts. Those closely related to human infancy, adapting and adjusting the child to the world in which he lives, may be called *adaptive*. There is still another group of inherited tendencies connected with sex and reproduction, which are not discussed in this book.

We shall give a brief discussion of the instincts falling under these various classes. It must be remembered, however, that the

47

psychology of the instincts is indefinite and obscure. It is difficult to bring the instincts into the laboratory for accurate study. For our knowledge of the instincts we are dependent, for the most part, on general observation. We have had a few careful studies of the very earliest years of childhood. However, although from the theoretical point of view our knowledge of the instincts is incomplete, it is sufficient to be of considerable practical value.

The Individualistic Instincts. Man's civilized life has covered but a short period of time, only a few hundred or a few thousand years. His pre-civilized life doubtless covered a period of millions of years. The inborn tendencies in us are such as were developed in the long period of savage life. During all of man's life in the time before civilization, he was always in danger. He had many enemies, and most of these enemies had the advantage of him in strength and natural means of defense. Unaided by weapons, he could hardly hold his own against any of the beasts of prey. So there were developed in man by the process of natural selection many inherited responses which we group under the head of *fear* responses.

Just what the various situations are that bring forth these responses has never been carefully worked out. But any situation that suddenly puts an individual in danger of losing his life brings about characteristic reactions. The most characteristic of the responses are shown in connection with circulation and respiration. Both of these processes are much interfered with. Sometimes the action is accelerated, at other times it is retarded, and in some cases the respiratory and cir culatory organs are almost paralyzed. Also the small muscles of the skin are made to contract, producing the sensation of the hair standing on end. Just what the original use of all these responses was it is difficult now to work out, but doubtless each served some useful purpose.

Whether any particular situations now call forth inherited fear responses in us is not definitely established. But among lower animals there are certain definite and particular situations which do call forth fear responses. On the whole, the evidence rather favors the idea of definite fear situations among children. It seems that certain situations do invariably arouse fear responses. To be alone in the dark, to be in a strange place, to hear loud and sudden noises, to see large, strange animals coming in threatening manner, seem universally to call forth fear responses in children.

However, the whole situation must always be considered. A situation in which the father or mother is present is quite different from one in which they are both absent. But it is certain that these and other fears are closely related to the age and development of the child. In the earlier years of infancy, certain fears are not present that are present later. And it can be demonstrated that the fears that do arise as infancy passes on are natural and inherited and not the result of experience.

Few of the original causes of fear now exist. The original danger was from wild animals chiefly. Seldom are we now in such danger. But of course this has been the case for only a short time. Our bodies are the same sort of bodies that our ancestors had, therefore we are full of needless fears. During the early years of a child's life, wise treatment causes most of the fear tendencies to disappear because of disuse. On the other hand, unwise treatment may accentuate and perpetuate them, causing much misery and unhappiness. Neither the home nor the school should play upon these ancestral fears. We should not try to get a child to be good by frightening him; nor should we often use fear of pain as an incentive to get a child to do his work.

Man has always been afraid, but he has also always been a fighter. He has always had to fight for his life against the lower animals, and he has also fought his fellow man. The fighting response is connected with the emotions of anger, envy, and jealousy. A man is angered by anything that interferes with his life, with his purposes, with whatever he calls his own. We become angry if some one strikes our bodies, or attacks our beliefs, or the beliefs of our dear friends, particularly of our families. The typical responses connected with anger are such as faster heart-beat, irregular breathing, congestion of the blood in the face and head, tightening of the voluntary muscles, particularly a setting of the teeth and a clinching of the fists. These responses are preparatory to actual combat.

Anger, envy, and jealousy, and the responses growing out of them, have always played a large part in the life of man. A great part of history is a record of the fights of nations, tribes, and individuals. If the records of wars and strifes, and the acts growing out of envy and jealousy and other similar emotions should be taken out of history, there would not be much left. Much of literature and art depict those actions of man which grew out of these individualistic aspects of his nature. Competition, which is an aspect of fighting, even to the present day, continues to be one of the main factors in business and in life generally. Briefly, fighting re sponses growing out of man's selfishness are as old as man himself, and the inherited tendencies connected with them are among the strongest of our natures.

In the training of children, one of the most difficult tasks is to help them to get control over the fighting instinct and other selfish tendencies. These tendencies are so deeply rooted in our natures that it is hard to get control of them. In fact, the control which we do get over them is always relative. The best we can hope to do is to get control over our fighting tendencies in ordinary circumstances.

It is doubtful whether it would be good for us if the fighting spirit should disappear from the race. It puts vim and determination into the life of man. But our fighting should not be directed against our fellow man. The fighting spirit can be retained and directed against evil and other obstacles. We can learn to attack our tasks in a fighting spirit. But surely the time has come when we should cease fighting against our neighbors.

Social Tendencies. Over against our fighting tendencies we may set the socialistic tendencies. Coöperative and sympathetic actions grow out of original nature, just as truly as do the selfish acts. But the socialistic tendencies are not, in general, as strong as are the individualistic ones. What society needs is the strengthening of the socialistic tendencies by use, and a weakening of at least some of the individualistic tendencies, by control and disuse.

Socialistic tendencies show themselves in gangs and clubs formed by children and adults. It is, therefore, a common practice now to speak of the "gang" instinct. Human beings are pleased and content when with other human beings and not content, not satisfied, when alone. Of course circumstances make a differ ence in the desires of men, but the general original tendency is as stated.

The gang of the modern city has the following explanation: Boys like to be with other boys. Moreover, they like to be active; they want to be doing something. The city does not provide proper means for the desired activities, such as hunting, fishing, tramping, and boating. It does not provide experiences with animals, such as boys have on the farm. Much of the boy's day is spent in school in a kind of work not at all like what he would do by choice. There is not much home life. Usually there is not the proper parental control. Seldom do the parents interest themselves in planning for the activities of their children. The result is that the boys come together on the streets and form a club or gang. Through this organization the boy's nature expresses itself. Without proper guidance from older people, this expression takes a direction not good for the future character and usefulness of the boy.

The social life of children should be provided for by the school in coöperation with the home. The school or the schoolroom should constitute a social unit. The teacher with the parents should plan the social life of the children. The actual work of the school can be very much socialized. There can be much more coöperation and much more group work can be done in the school than is the case at present. And many other social activities can be organized in connection with the school and its work. Excursions, pageants, shows, picnics, and all sorts of activities should be undertaken.

The schoolhouse should be used by the community as the place for many of its social acts and performances. Almost every night, and throughout the summer as well as in the winter, the people, young and old, should meet at the school for some sort of social work or play. The Boy Scouts should be brought under the control of the school to help fulfill some of its main purposes.

Environmental Instincts. In this class there are at least two tendencies which seem to be part of the original nature of man; namely, the *wandering* and the *collecting* tendencies.

Wandering. The long life that our ancestors lived free and unrestrained in the woods has left its effect within us. One of the greatest achievements of civilization has been to overcome the inherited tendencies to roam and wander, to the extent that for the most part we live out our lives in one home, in one family, doing often but one kind of work all our lives. Originally, man had much more freedom to come and go and do whatever he wished.

Truancies and runaways are the result of original tendencies and desires expressing themselves in spite of training, perhaps sometimes because of the lack of training. In childhood and youth these original tendencies should, to some extent, be satisfied in legitimate ways. Excursions and picnics can be planned both for work and for play. If the child's desires and needs can be satisfied in legitimate ways, then he will not have to satisfy them illegitimately. The teaching itself can be done better by following, to some extent, the lead of the child's nature. Much early education consists in learning the world. Now, most of the world is out of doors and the child must go out to find it. The teacher should make use of the natural desires of the children to wander and explore, as a means of educating them. The school work should be of such a nature that much outdoor work will need to be done.

Collecting. It is in the nature of children to seize and, if possible, carry away whatever attracts attention. This tendency is the basis of what is called the collecting instinct. If one will take a walk with a child, one can observe the operation of the collecting tendency, particularly if the walk is in the fields and woods. The child will be observed to take leaves, flowers, fruits, seeds, nuts, pebbles, and in fact everything that is loose or can be gotten loose. They are taken at first aimlessly, merely because they attract attention. The original, natural response of the child toward that which attracts attention is usually to get it, get possession of it and take it along. It is easy to see why such tendencies were developed in man. In his savage state it was highly useful for him to do this. He must always have been on the lookout for things which could be used as food or as weapons. He had to do this to live. But one need not take a child to the woods to observe this tendency. One can go to the stores. Till a child is trained not to do it, he seizes and takes whatever attracts attention.

Just as the wandering tendencies can be used for the benefit of the child, so can the collecting tendencies. Not only should the children make expeditions to learn of the world, but specimens should be collected so that they can be used to form a museum at the school which will represent the surrounding locality. Geological, geographical, botanical, and zoölogical specimens should be collected. The children will learn much while making the collections, and much from the collections after they are made.

"Education could profit greatly by making large demands upon the collecting instinct. It seems clear that in their childhood is the time when children should be sent forth to the fields and woods, to study what they find there and to gather specimens. The children can form naturalists' clubs for the purpose of studying the natural environment. Such study should embrace rocks, soils, plants, leaves, flowers, fruits, and specimens of the wood of the various trees. Birds and insects can be studied and collected. The work of such a club would have a twofold value. (1) The study and collecting acquaint the child with his natural environment, and in doing it, afford a sphere for the activity of many aspects of his nature. They take him out of doors and give an opportunity for exploring every nook and corner of the natural environment. The collecting can often be done in such a way as to appeal to the group instincts. For example, the club could hold meetings for exhibiting and studying the specimens, and sometimes the actual collecting could be done in groups. (2) The specimens collected should be put into the school museum, and the aim of this museum should be to represent completely the local environment, the natural and physical environment, and also the industrial, civil, and social environment. The museum should be completely illustrative of the child's natural, physical, and social surroundings. The museum would therefore be educative in its making, and when it is made, it would have immense value to the community, not only to the children but to all the people. In this museum, of course, should be found the minerals, rocks, soils, insects,—particularly those of economic importance,—birds, and also specimens of the wild animals of the locality. If proper appeal is made to the natural desire of the children, this instinct would soon be made of service in producing a very valuable collection. The school museum in which these specimens are placed should also include other classes of specimens. There should be specimens showing industrial evolution, the stages of manufacture of raw material, specimens of local historical interest, pictures, documents, books. The museum should be made of such a nature that parents would go there nearly as often as the children. The school should be for the instruction of all the people of the community. It should be the experiment station, the library, the debating club, the art gallery for the whole community."

Imitation. One of the fundamental original traits of human nature is the tendency to imitate. Imitation is not instinctive in the strict meaning of the word. Seeing a certain act performed does not, apart from training and experience, serve as a stimulus to make a child perform a similar act. Hearing a certain sound does not serve as a stimulus for the production of the same sound. Nevertheless, there is in the human child a tendency or desire to do what it sees others doing.

A few hours spent in observing children ought to convince any one of the universality and of the strength of this tendency. As our experience becomes organized, the idea of an act usually serves as the stimulus to call it forth. However, this is not because the idea of an act, of necessity, always produces the act. It is merely a matter of the stimulus and the response *becoming connected in that way* as the result of experience. Our meaning is that an act can be touched off or prompted by any stimulus. Our nervous organization makes this possible. The particular stimulus that calls forth a particular response depends upon how we have been trained, how we have learned. In most cases our acts are coupled up with the ideas of the acts. We learn them that way.

In early life particularly, the connection between stimulus and response is very close. When a child gets the idea of an act, he immediately performs the act, if he knows how. Now, seeing another perform an act brings the act clearly into the child's consciousness, and he proceeds to perform it. But the act must be one which the child already knows how to perform, otherwise his performance of it will be faulty and incomplete. If he has never performed the particular act, seeing another perform the act sets him to trying to do it and he may soon learn it. If he successfully performs an act when he sees it done by another, the act must be one which he already knows how to perform, and for whose performance the idea has already served as a stimulus. Now if imitation were instinctive in the strict sense, one could perform the act for the first time merely from seeing another do it, without any previous experience or learning. It is doubtful whether there are any such inherited connections. It is, however, true that human beings are of such a nature that, particularly in early life, they *like* to do and *want* to do what they see others doing. This is one of the most important aspects of human nature, as we shall see.

Function and Importance of Imitation in Life. Natural selection has developed few aspects of human nature so important for survival as the tendency to imitate, for this tendency quickly leads to a successful adjustment of the child to the world in which he lives. Adult men and women are successfully adjusted to their environment. Their adjustment might be better, but it is good enough to keep them alive for a time. Now, if children do as they see their parents doing, they will reach a satisfactory adjustment.

We may, therefore, say that the tendency to imitate serves to adjust the child to his environment. It is for this reason that imitation has been called an *adaptive instinct*. It would perhaps be better to say merely that the *tendency* to imitate is part of the *original equipment of man*.

Imitation is distinctively a human trait. While it occurs in lower animals it is probably not an important factor in adjusting them to their environment. But in the human race it is one of the chief factors in adjustment to environment. Imitation is one of the main factors in education. Usually the quickest way to teach a child to do a thing is to show him how.

Through imitation we acquire our language, manners, and customs. Ideals, beliefs, prejudices, attitudes, we take on through imitation. The tendency to imitate others coupled with the desire to be thought well of by others is one of the most powerful factors in producing conformity. They are the whips which keep us within the bounds of custom and conventionality. The tendency to imitate is so strong that its results are almost as certain as are those of inherited tendencies. It is almost as certain that a child will be like his parents in speech, manners, customs, superstitions, etc., as it is that he will be like them in form of body. He not only walks and talks and acts like his parents, but he thinks as they do. We, therefore, have the term *social heredity*, meaning the taking on of all sorts of social habits and ideals through imitation.

The part that imitation plays in the education of a child may be learned by going to a country home and noting how the boy learns to do all the many things about the farm by imitating his father, and how the girl learns to do all the housework by imitating her mother. Imitation is the basis of much of the play of children, in that their play consists in large part of doing what they see older people doing. This imitative play gives them skill and is a large factor in preparing for the work of life.

Dramatization. Dramatization is an aspect of imitation, and is a means of making ideas more real than they would otherwise be.

There is nothing that leads us so close to reality as action. We never completely know an act till we have done it. Dramatization is a matter of carrying an idea out into action. Ideas give to action its greatest fullness of meaning.

Dramatic representation should, therefore, have a prominent place in the schools, particularly in the lower grades. If the child is allowed to mimic the characters in the reading lesson, the meaning of the lesson becomes fuller. Later on in the school course, dramatic representation of the characters in literature and history is a means of getting a better conception of these characters. In geography, the study of the manners and customs and occupations of foreign peoples can be much facilitated through dramatic representation. Children naturally have the dramatic tendency; it is one aspect of the tendency to imitate. We have only to encourage it and make use of it throughout the school course.

Imitation in Ideals. Imitation is of importance not only in acquiring the actions of life but also in getting our ideals. Habits of thinking are no less an aspect of our lives than are habits of acting. Our attitudes, our prejudices, our beliefs, our moral, religious, and political ideals are in large measure copied from people about us. The family and social atmosphere in which one lives is a mold in which one's mind is formed and shaped. We cannot escape the influence of this atmosphere if we would. One takes on a belief that his father has, one clings to this belief and interprets the world in the light of it. This belief becomes a part of one's nature. It is a mental habit, a way of looking at the world. It is as much a part of one as red hair or big feet or a crooked nose. Probably no other influence has so much to do with making us what we are as social beings as the influence of imitation.

Play. Play is usually considered to be a part of the original equipment of man. It is essentially an expression of the ripening instincts of children, and not a specific instinct itself. It is rather a sort of make-believe activity of all the instincts. Kittens and dogs may be seen in play to mimic fighting. They bite and chew each other as in real fighting, but still they are not fighting.

As the structures and organs of children mature, they demand activity. This early activity is called play. It has several characteristics. The main one is that it is pleasurable. Play activity is pleasurable in itself. We do not play that we may get something else which we like, as is the case with the activity which we call work. Play is an end in itself. It is not a means to get something else which is intrinsically valuable.

One of the chief values of play comes from its activity aspect. We are essentially motor beings. We grow and develop only through exercise. In early life we do not have to exert ourselves to get a living. Play is nature's means of giving our organs the exercise which they must have to bring them to maturity. Play is an expression of the universal tendency to action in early life. Without play, the child would not develop, would not become a normal human being.

All day long the child is ceaselessly active. The value of this activity can hardly be overestimated. It not only leads to healthy growth, but is a means through which the child learns himself and the world. Everything that the child sees excites him to react to it or upon it. He gets possession of it. He bites it. He pounds it. He throws it. In this way he learns the properties of things and the characteristics of forces. Through play and imitation, in a very few years the child comes to a successful adjustment in his world.

Play and imitation are the great avenues of activity in early life. Even in later life, we seldom accomplish anything great or worth while until the thing becomes play to us, until we throw our whole being into it as we do in play, until it is an expression of ourselves as play is in our childhood. The proper use of play gives us the solution of many of the problems of early education.

Play has two functions in the school: (1) Motor play is necessary to growth, development, and health. The constant activity of the child is what brings about healthy growth.

In the country it is not difficult for children to get plenty of the proper kind of exercise, but in the larger cities it is difficult. Nevertheless, opportunity for play should be provided for every child, no matter what the trouble or expense, for without play children cannot become normal human beings. Everywhere parents and teachers should plan for the play life of the children.

(2) In the primary grades play can have a large place in the actual work of the school. The early work of education is to a large extent getting the tools of knowledge and thought and work—reading, spelling, writing, correct speech, correct writing, the elementary processes of arithmetic, etc. In many ways play can be used in acquiring these tools.

One aspect of play particularly should have a large place in education; namely, the manipulative tendencies of children. This is essentially play. Children wish to handle and manipulate everything that attracts their attention. They wish to tear it to pieces and to put it together. This is nature's way of teaching, and by it children learn the properties and structures of things. They thereby learn what things do and what can be done with them. Teachers and parents should foster these manipulative tendencies and use them for the child's good. These tendencies are an aspect of curiosity. We want to know. We are unhappy as long as a thing is before us which we do not understand, which has some mystery about it. Nature has developed these tendencies in us, for without a knowledge of our surroundings we could not live. The child therefore has in his nature the basis of his education. We have but to know this nature and wisely use and manipulate it to achieve the child's education.

SUMMARY. Instincts are inherited tendencies to specific actions. They fall under the heads: individualistic, socialistic, environmental, adaptive, sexual or mating instincts. These inherited tendencies are to a large extent the foundation on which we build education. The educational problem is to control and guide them, suppressing some, fostering others. In everything we undertake for a child we must take into account these instincts.

CLASS EXERCISES

1.   Make a study of the instincts of several animals, such as dogs, cats, chickens. Make a list showing the stimuli and the inherited responses.

2.   Make a study of the instincts of a baby. See how many inherited responses you can observe. The simpler inherited responses are known as *reflexes*. The closing of the eyelids mentioned in the text is an example. How many such reflexes can you find in a child?

3.   Make a special study of the fears of very young children. How many definite situations can you find which excite fear responses in all children? Each member of the class can make a list of his own fears. It may then be seen whether any fears are common to all members of the class and whether there are any sex differences.

4.   Similarly, make a study of anger and fighting. What situations invariably arouse the fighting response? In what definite, inherited ways is anger shown? Do your studies and observations convince you that the fighting instinct and other inherited responses concerned with individual survival are among the strongest of inherited tendencies? Can the fighting instinct be eliminated from the human race? Is it desirable to eliminate it?

5.   Make a study of children's collections. Take one of the grades and find what collections the children have made. What different objects are collected?

6.   Outline a plan for using the collecting instinct in various school studies.

7.   With the help of the principal of the school make a study of some specific cases of truancy. What does your finding show?

8.   Make a study of play by watching children of various ages play. Make a list of the games that are universal for infancy, those

for childhood, and those for youth. (Consult Johnson's *Plays and Games*.)

9.   What are the two main functions of play in education? Why should we play after we are mature?

10.   Study imitation in very young children. Do this by watching the spontaneous play of children under six. What evidences of imitation do you find?

11.   Outline the things we learn by imitation. What is your opinion of the place which imitation has in our education?

12.   Make a study of imitation as a factor in the lives of grown people. Consider styles, fashions, manners, customs, beliefs, prejudices, religious ideas, etc.

13.   On the whole, is imitation a good thing or a bad thing?

14.   Make a plan of the various ways in which dramatization can be profitably used in the schools.

15.   Make a study of your own ideals. What ideals do you have? Where did you get them? What ideals did you get from your parents? What from books? What from teachers? What from friends?

16.   Show that throughout life inherited tendencies are the fundamental bases from which our actions proceed, on which our lives are erected.

17.   Make a complete outline of the chapter.

REFERENCES FOR CLASS READING

- COLVIN and BAGLEY: *Human Behavior*, Chapters III, VIII, IX, and X.

- KIRKPATRICK: *Fundamentals of Child Study*, Chapters IV–XIII.

- MÜNSTERBERG: *Psychology, General and Applied*, pp. 184–187.

- PILLSBURY: *Essentials of Psychology*, Chapter X.

- PYLE: *The Outlines of Educational Psychology*, Chapters IV–IX.

- TITCHENER: *A Beginner's Psychology*, Chapter VIII.

CHAPTER V

FEELING AND ATTENTION

The Feelings. Related to the instincts on one side and to habits on the other are the feelings. In Chapter III we discussed sensation, and in the preceding chapter, the instincts, but when we have described an act in terms of instinct and sensation, we have not told all the facts.

For example, when a child sees a pretty red ball of yarn, he reaches out to get it, then puts it into his mouth, or unwinds it, and plays with it in various ways. It is all a matter of sensation and instinctive responses. The perception of the ball—seeing the ball—brings about the instinctive reaching out, grasping the ball, and bringing it to the mouth. But to complete our account, we must say that the child is *pleased*. We note a change in his facial expression. His eyes gleam with pleasure. His face is all smiles, showing pleasant contentment. Therefore we must say that the child not only sees, not only acts, but the seeing and acting are *pleasant*. The child continues to look, he continues to act, because the looking and acting bring joy.

This is typical of situations that bring pleasure. We want them continued; we act in a way to make them continue. *We go out after the pleasure-giving thing.*

But let us consider a different kind of situation. A child sees on the hearth a glowing coal. It instinctively reaches out and grasps it, starts to draw the coal toward it, but instinctively drops it. This is not, however, the whole story. Instead of the situation being pleasant, it is decidedly unpleasant. The child fairly howls with pain. His face, instead of being wreathed in smiles, is covered with tears. He did not hold on to the coal. He did not try to continue the situation. On the contrary, he dropped the coal, and withdrew the hand. The body contracted and shrank away from the situation.

These two cases illustrate the two simple feelings, pleasantness and unpleasantness. Most situations in life are either pleasant or unpleasant. Situations may sometimes be neutral; that is, may arouse neither the feeling of pleasantness or unpleasantness. But usually a conscious state is either pleasant or unpleasant. A situation brings us life, joy, happiness. We want it continued and act in a way to bring about its continuance. Or the situation tends to take away our life, brings pain, sorrow, grief, and we want it discontinued, and act in a way to discontinue it.

These two simple forms of feeling perhaps arose in the beginning in connection with the act of taking food. It is known that if a drop of acid touches an amœba, the animal shrinks, contracts, and tries to withdraw from the death-bringing acid. On the other hand, if a particle of a substance that is suitable for food touches the animal, it takes the particle within itself. The particle is life-giving and brings pleasure.

The Emotions. Pleasure and displeasure are the simple feelings. Most situations in life bring about very complex feeling states known as *emotions*. The emotions are made up of pleasure or displeasure mixed or compounded with the sensations from the bodily reactions.

The circulatory system, the respiratory system, and nearly all the involuntary organs of the body form a great sounding board which instantly responds in various ways to the situations of life. When the youth sees the pretty maiden and when he touches her hand, his heart pumps away at a great rate, his cheeks become flushed, his breathing is paralyzed, his voice trembles. He experiences the emotion of love. The state is complex indeed. There is pleasantness, of course, but there is in addition the feeling of all the bodily reactions.

When the mother sees her dead child lying in its casket, her head falls over on her breast, her eyes fill with tears, her shoulders droop, her chest contracts, she sobs, her breathing is spasmodic. Nearly every organ of the body is affected in one way or another.

The state is *unpleasant,* but there is also the feeling of the manifold bodily reactions.

So it is always. The biologically important situations in life bring about, through hereditary connections in the nervous system, certain typical reactions. These reactions are largely the same for the same type of situation, and they give the particular coloring to each emotion. It is evident that the emotions are closely related to the instincts. The reflexes that take place in emotions are of the same nature as the instincts. Each instinctive act has its characteristic emotion. There are fear instincts and fear emotions. Fear is unpleasant. In addition to its unpleasantness there is a multitude of sensations that come from the body. The hair stands on end, the heart throbs, the circulation is hastened, breathing is interrupted, the muscles are tense. This peculiar mass of sensations, blended with the unpleasantness, gives the characteristic emotion of fear. But we need not go into an analysis of the various emotions of love, hate, envy, grief, jealousy, etc. The reader can do this for himself.

Nearly every organ of the body plays its part in the emotions: the digestive organs, the liver, the kidneys, the throat and mouth, the salivary glands, the eyes and tear glands, the skin muscles, the facial muscles, etc. And every emotion is made up of pleasantness or unpleasantness and the sensations produced by some combination of bodily reactions.

It is well for us to remember the part that bodily conditions and states play in the emotional life. The emotional state of a man depends upon whether he has had his dinner or is hungry, whether the liver is working normally, and upon the condition of the various secreting and excreting organs and glands. In a word, it is evident that our emotions fall within a world of cause and effect. *Our feeling states are caused.*

Importance in Life. Our feelings and emotions are the fountains from which nearly all our volitional actions flow. Feeling is the *mainspring* of life. Nearly everything we do is prompted by love, or hate, or fear, or jealousy, or rivalry, or anger, or grief. If the feelings have such close relation to action, then the schools must take them into account, for by education we seek to control action. If the feelings control action, then we must try to control the feelings. We must get the child into a right state of mind toward the school, toward his teacher, and toward his work. The child must like the school, like the teacher, and *want* to learn.

Moreover, we must create the right state of mind in connection with each study, each task. The child must come to feel the need and importance of each individual task as well as of each subject. The task is then desirable, it is to be sought for and worked at, it is important for life.

This is merely enlisting the child's nature in the interest of his education. For motive, we must always look to the child's nature. The two great forces which pull and drive are *pleasure* and *pain*. Nature has no other methods. Formerly the school used pain as its motive almost exclusively. The child did his tasks to escape pain. For motive we now use more often the positive influences which give pleasure, which pull instead of drive. What will one not do *for* the *loved* one? What will one not do *to* the *hated* one? The child who does not love his teacher gets little good from school while under that teacher. Moreover, school work is often a failure because it is so unreal, has so little relation to an actual world, and seems foreign to any real needs of the child. No one is going to work very hard unless the work is prompted by desire. Our desires come from our needs. Therefore, if we are to enlist the child's feelings in the service of his education, we must make the school work vital and relate it, if possible, to the actual needs of the child.

It must not be forgotten, however, that we must build up permanent attitudes of respect for authority, obedience, and reverence for the important things of life. Neither must it be forgotten that we can create needs in the child. If in the education of the child we follow only such needs as he has, we will make a fine savage of him but nothing else. It is the business of the school to create in the child the right kind of needs. As was pointed out in our study of the instincts, we must make the child over again into what he ought to be. But this cannot be a sudden process. One cannot arouse enthusiasm in a six-year-old child over the beauties of higher mathematics. It takes ten or fifteen years to do that, and it must be done little by little.

Control of the Emotions. Without training, we remain at the mercy of our baser emotions. The child must be trained to control himself. Here is where habit comes in to modify primitive action. The child can be trained to inhibit or prevent the reactions that arise in hatred, envy, jealousy, anger, etc. For a fuller discussion of this point we must wait till we come to the discussion of habit and moral training.

Mood and Temperament. A mood is a somewhat extended emotional state continuing for hours or days. It is due to a continuance of the factors which cause it. The state of the liver and digestive organs may throw one for days into a cross and ugly mood. When the body becomes normal, the mood changes or disappears. Similarly, one may for hours or days be overjoyed, or depressed, or morose, or melancholy. Parents and teachers should look well to the matter of creating and establishing continuous and permanent states of feeling that are favorable to work and development.

Some people are permanently optimistic, others pessimistic. Some are always joyful, others as constantly see only the dark side of life. Some are always serious and solemn, others always gay, even giddy. These permanent emotional attitudes constitute temperament, and are due to fundamental differences within the body that are in some cases hereditary. Crossness and moroseness, for example, may be due to a dyspeptic condition and a chronically bad liver. The happy dispositions belong to bodies whose organs are func tioning properly, in which assimilation is good—all the parts of the body doing their proper work.

Poor eyes which are under a constant strain, through the reflex effects upon various organs of the body, are likely to develop a permanently cross and irritable disposition. Through the close sympathetic relation of the various organs, anything affecting one organ and interfering with its proper action is likely to affect many other organs and profoundly influence the emotional states of the body. In growing children particularly, there are many influences which affect their emotions, things of which we seldom think, such as the condition of vision and hearing, the condition of the teeth, nose, and throat, and the condition of all the important vital organs of the body. When a child's disposition is not what we think it ought to be, we should try to find out the causes.

Training the Emotions. The emotions are subject to training. The child can be taught control. Moreover, he can be taught to appreciate and enjoy higher things than mere animal pleasure; namely, art, literature, nature, truth. The child thereby becomes a spiritual being instead of a mere pig. The ideal of the school should be to develop men and women whose baser passions are under control, who are calm, self-controlled, and self-directed, and who get their greatest pleasure from the finer and higher things of life, such as the various forms of music, the songs of birds, the beauties and intricate workings of nature.

This is a wonderful world and a wonderful life, but the child may go through the world without seeing it, and live his life without knowing what it is to live. His eyes must be opened, he must be trained to see and to feel. It is not the place here to tell how this is to be done. This is not a book on methods of teaching. We can only indicate here that the business of the school is not merely to teach people how to make a living, but to teach them how to enjoy the living. There are many avenues from which we get the higher forms of pleasure. There are really many different worlds which we may experience: the world of animals, the world of plants, the mechanical world, the chemical world, the world of literature and of art, the world of music. It is the duty of the schools to open up these worlds to the children, and make them so many possibilities of joy and happiness.

The emotions and feelings, then, are not lawless and causeless, but are a part of a world of law and order. They are themselves caused and therefore subject to control and modification.

Attention. Attention, too, is related to inherited tendencies on the one side and to habits on the other. If one is walking in the woods and catches a glimpse of something moving in the trees, the eyes *instinctively* turn so that the person can get a better view of the object. If one hears a sudden sound, the head is instinctively turned so that the person can hear better. One stops, the body is held still and rigid, breathing is slow and controlled—all to favor better hearing.

The various acts of attention are reflex and instinctive. But what is attention? By attention we mean *sensory clearness*. When we say we are attentive to a thing or subject, we mean that perceptions or ideas of that thing or subject are *clear* as compared to other perceptions and ideas that are in consciousness at the same time. The contents of one's consciousness, the perceptions and ideas that constitute one's mind at any one moment are always arranged in an *attentive* pattern, some being clear, others unclear. The pattern constantly changes and shifts. What is now clear and in the focus of consciousness, presently is unclear and may in a moment disappear from consciousness altogether, while other perceptions or ideas take its place.

The first question that arises in connection with attention is, What are the causes of attention? The first group of causes are hereditary and instinctive. The child attends to loud things, bright things, moving things, etc. But as we grow older, the basis of attention becomes more and more *habit*. An illustration will make this clear. I once spent a day at a great exposition with a machinist. He was constantly attending to things mechanical, when I would not even see them. He had spent many years working with machinery, and as a result, things mechanical at once attracted him. Similarly, if a man and a woman walk along a street together and look in at the shop windows, the woman sees only hats, dresses, ribbons, and other finery, while the man sees only cigars, pipes, and automobile supplies. Every day we live, we are building up habits of attending to certain types of things. What repeatedly comes into our experience, easily attracts our attention to the exclusion of other things.

The Function of Attention. Attention is the unifying aspect of consciousness. There are always many things in consciousness, and we cannot respond to all at once. The part of consciousness that is clear and focal brings about action. The things to which we attend are the things that count.

In later chapters we shall learn that in habit-formation, attention is an important factor. We must attend to the acts we are trying to make habitual. In getting knowledge, we must attend to what we are trying to learn. In committing to memory, we must attend to the ideas that we are trying to fix and make permanent. In thinking and reasoning, those ideas become associated together that are together in attention.

Attention is therefore the controlling aspect of consciousness. It is the basis of what we call *will*. The ideas that are clear and focal and that persist in consciousness are the ideas that control our action. When one says he has made up his mind, he has made a choice; that merely means that a certain group of ideas persist in consciousness to the exclusion of others. These are the ideas which ultimately produce action. And it is our past experience that determines what ideas will become focal and persist.

Training the Attention. There are two aspects of the training of attention. (1) We can learn to hold ourselves to a task. When we sit down to a table to study, there may be many things that tend to call us away. There lies a magazine which we might read, there is a play at the theater, there are noises outside, there is a friend calling across the street. But we must study. We have set ourselves to a task and we must hold fast to our purpose.

The young child cannot do this. He must be trained to do it. The instruments used to train him are pleasure and pain, rewards and punishments that come from parents. Gradually, slowly, the child gains control over himself. No one ever amounts to anything till he can hold himself to a task, to a fixed purpose. One must learn to form plans extending over weeks, months, and years, and to hold unflinchingly to them, just as one must hold himself to his study table and allow nothing to distract or to interfere. No training a child can receive is more important than this, for it gives him control over his life, it gives him control over the ideas that are to become focal and determine action. It is for this reason that we call such training a training of attention. It might perhaps better be called a training of the will. But the will is only the attentive consciousness. The idea that is clear, that holds its own in consciousness, is the idea that produces action. When we say that we *will* to do a certain thing, all we can mean is that the *idea of this act* is clearest and holds its focal place in consciousness to the exclusion of other ideas. It therefore goes over into action.

(2) The training just discussed may be called a general training of attention giving us a general power and control over our lives, but there is another type of training which is specific. As with the machinist mentioned above, so with all of us; we attend to the type of thing that we have formed a habit of attending to. Continued experience in a certain field makes it more and more easy to attend to things in that field. One can take a certain subject and work at it day after day, year after year. By and by, the whole world takes on the aspect of this chosen subject. The entomologist sees bugs everywhere, the botanist sees only plants, the mechanic sees only machines, the preacher sees only the moral and religious aspects of action, the doctor sees only disease, the mathematician sees always the quantitative aspect of things. Ideas and perceptions related to one's chosen work go at once and readily to the focus of consciousness; other things escape notice.

It is for this reason that we become "crankier" every year that we live. We are attending to only one aspect of the world. While this blinds us to other aspects of the world, it brings mastery in our individual fields. We can, then, by training and practice, get a general control over attention, and by working in a certain field or kind of work, we make it easy to attend to things in that field or work. This to an extent gives us control of our lives, of our destiny.

Interest. The essential elements of interest are attention and feeling. When a person is very attentive to a subject and gets pleasure from experience in that subject, we commonly say that he is *interested* in that subject.

Since the importance of attention and feeling in learning has already been shown and will be further developed in the chapters which follow in connection with the subjects of habit, memory, and thinking, little more need be said here.

The key to all forms of learning is *attention*. The key to attention is *feeling*. Feeling depends upon the nature of the child, inherited and acquired. In our search for the means of arousing interest, we look first to the original nature of the child, to the instincts and the emotions. We look next to the acquired nature, the habits, the ideals, the various needs that have grown up in the individual's life. Educational writers have overemphasized the original nature of the child as a basis of interest and have not paid enough attention to acquired nature. We should not ask so much what a child's needs are, but what they *ought* to be. Needs can be created. The child's nature to some extent can be changed. The problem of arousing interest is therefore one of finding in the child's nature a basis for attention and pleasure. If the basis is not to be found there, then it must be built up. How this can be done, how human nature can be changed, is to some extent the main problem of psychology. Every chapter in this book, it is hoped, will be found to throw some light on the problem.

SUMMARY. The two elementary feeling states are pleasantness and unpleasantness. The emotions are complex mental states composed of feeling and the sensations from bodily reactions to the situations. Feeling and emotion are the motive forces of life, at the bottom of all important actions. The bodily reactions of emotions are reflex and instinctive. Attention is a matter of the relative clearness of the contents of consciousness. The function of attention is to unify thought and action. It is the important factor in all learning and thinking, for it is only the attentive part of consciousness that is effective.

CLASS EXERCISES

1.   Make out a complete list of the more important emotions.

2.   Indicate the characteristic expression of each emotion in your list.

3.   Can you have an emotion without its characteristic expression? If, for example, when a situation arises which ordinarily arouses anger in you, you inhibit all the usual motor accompaniments of anger, are you really angry?

4.   Are the expressions of the same emotion the same for all people?

5.   Try to analyze some of your emotional states: anger, or fear, or grief. Can you detect the sensations that come from the bodily reactions?

6.   Try to induce an emotional state by producing its characteristic reactions.

7.   Try to change an emotional state to an opposite emotion; for example, grief to joy.

8.   Try to control and change emotional states in children.

9.   Name some sensations that for you are always pleasant, others that are always unpleasant—colors, sounds, tastes, odors, temperatures.

10.   Confirm by observation the statement of the text as to the importance of emotions in all the important actions of life.

11.   To what extent do you have control of your emotional states? What have you observed about differences in expression of deep emotions by different people? In case of death in the family, some people wail and moan and express their grief in the most extreme manner, while others do not utter a sound and show great control. Why the difference?

12.   Make an introspective study of your conscious states to note the difference in clearness of the different processes that are going on in consciousness. Do you find a constant shifting?

13.   Perform experiments to show the effects of attention in forming habits and acquiring knowledge.

a.   Perform tests in learning, using substitution tests as described in Chapter X. Use several different keys. In some experiments have no distractions, in others, have various distracting noises. What differences do you find in the results?

b.   Try learning nonsense syllables, some lists with distractions, others without distractions.

c.   Try getting the ideas from stories read to you, as in the logical memory experiment described in Chapter X. Some stories should be read without distractions, others with distractions.

14.   Why are you unable to study well when under the influence of some strong emotion?

15.   Are you trained to the extent that you can concentrate on a task and hold yourself to it for a long time?

16.   Do you see that as far as will and attention and the emotions are concerned, your life and character are in large measure in your own hands?

17.   Make a complete outline of the chapter.

REFERENCES FOR CLASS READING

- COLVIN and BAGLEY: *Human Behavior,* Chapters IV, V, and VI.

- MÜNSTERBERG: *Psychology, General and Applied,* Chapter XIV, also pp. 187–192 and pp. 370–371.

- PILLSBURY: *Essentials of Psychology,* Chapters V and XI.

- PYLE: *The Outlines of Educational Psychology,* Chapter XIV.

- TITCHENER: *A Beginner's Psychology,* Chapters IV, VIII, and XI.

CHAPTER VI

HABIT

The Nature of Habit. We now turn from man's inherited nature to his acquired nature. Inherited tendencies to action we have called instincts; acquired tendencies to action we shall call habits. We can best form an idea of the nature of habit by considering some concrete cases.

Let us take first the case of a man forming the habit of turning out the basement light. It usually happens that when a man has an electric light in the basement of his house, it is hard for him at first to think to turn out the light at night when he retires, and as a consequence the light often burns all night. This is expensive and unnecessary, so there is a strong incentive for the man to find a plan which will insure the regular turning-off of the light at bedtime. The plan usually hit upon is the following: The electric switch that controls the basement light is beside the basement stairway. The man learns to look at the switch as he comes up the stairs, after preparing the furnace fire for the night, and learns to take hold of the switch when he sees it and turn off the light. Coming up the stairs means to look at the switch. Seeing the switch means to turn it. Each step of the performance touches off the next. The man sees that in order to make sure that the light will always be turned off, the acts must all be made automatic, and each step must touch off the next in the series. At first, the man leaves the light burning about as often as he turns it off. After practicing for a time on the scheme, the different acts become so well connected that he seldom leaves the light burning. We say that he has formed the *habit* of turning off the light.

For a second illustration, let us take the process of learning that nine times nine equals eighty-one. At first, one does not say or write "eighty-one" when one sees "nine times nine," but one can acquire the habit of doing so. It does not here concern us how the child learns what the product of nine times nine is. He may learn it by counting, by being told, or by reading it in a book. But however he first learns it, he fixes it and makes it automatic and habitual by *continuing* to say or to write, "nine times nine equals eighty-one." The essential point is that at first the child does not know what to say when he hears or sees the expression "nine times nine," but after long practice he comes to give automatically and promptly the correct answer. For the definite problem "nine times nine" there comes the definite response "eighty-one."

For a third illustration, let us take the case of a man tipping his hat when he meets a lady. A young boy does not tip his hat when he meets a lady until he has been taught to do so. After he learns this act of courtesy he does it quite automatically without thinking of it. For the definite situation, meeting a lady of his acquaintance, there comes to be established the definite response, tipping the hat. A similar habit is that of turning to the right when we meet a person. For the definite situation, meeting a person on the road or street or sidewalk, there is established the definite re sponse, turning to the right. The response becomes automatic, immediate, certain.

There is another type of habit that may properly be called an intellectual habit, such as voting a certain party ticket, say the Democratic. When one is a boy, one hears his father speak favorably of the Democratic party. His father says, "Hurrah for Bryan," so he comes to say, "Hurrah for Bryan." His father says, "I am a Democrat," so he says he is a Democrat. He takes the side that his father takes. In a similar way we take on the same religious notions that our parents have. It does not always happen this way, but this is the rule. But no matter how we come to do it, we do adopt the creed of some party or some church. We adopt a certain way of looking at public questions, and a certain way of looking at religious questions. For certain rather definite situations, we come to take definite stands. When we go to the booth to vote, we look at the top of the ballot to find the column marked "Democratic," and the definite response is to check the "Democrat" column. Of course, some of us form a different habit and check the "Republican" column, but the psychology of the act is the same. The point is that we form the Democratic habit or we form the Republican habit; and the longer we practice the habit, the harder it is to change it.

In the presidential campaign of 1912, Roosevelt "bolted" from the Republican party. It was hard for the older Republicans to follow him. While one occasionally found a follower of Roosevelt who was gray, one usually found the old Republicans standing by the old party, the younger ones joining the Progressive party. It is said that when Darwin published "The Origin of Species," very few old men accepted the doc trine of evolution. The adherents of the new doctrine were nearly all young men. So there is such a thing as an intellectual habit. One comes to take a definite stand when facing certain definite intellectual situations.

Similar to the type of habits which we have called intellectual is another type which may be called "moral." When we face the situation of reporting an occurrence, we can tell the truth or we can lie. We can build up the habit of meeting such situations by telling the truth on all occasions. We can learn to follow the maxim "Tell the truth at all times, at all hazards." We can come to do this automatically, certainly, and without thought of doing anything else.

Most moral situations are fairly definite and clear-cut, and for them we can establish definite forms of response. We can form the habit of helping a person in distress, of helping a sick neighbor, of speaking well of a neighbor; we can form habits of industry, habits of perseverance. These and other similar habits are the basis of morality.

The various kinds of habits which we have enumerated are alike in certain fundamental particulars. In all of them there is a definite situation followed by a definite response. One sees the switch and turns off the light; he sees the expression "nine times nine" and says "eighty-one"; he sees a lady he knows and tips his hat; in meeting a carriage on the road, he turns to the right; when he has to vote, he votes a certain ticket; when he has to report an occurrence, he tells it as it happened. There is, in every case, a definite situation followed by a definite response.

Another characteristic is common to all the cases mentioned above, *i.e.* the response is acquired, it does not come at first. In every instance we might have learned to act differently. We could form the habit of always leaving the light burning; could just as easily say "nine times nine equals forty"; we could turn to the left; we could vote the Republican ticket. We can form bad moral habits as well as good ones, perhaps more easily. The point is, however, that we acquire definite ways of acting for the same situations, and these definite ways of acting are called habits.

Habit and Nerve-Path. It has already been stated that a habit is a tendency toward a certain type of action in a certain situation. The basis of this tendency is in the nervous system. In order to understand it we must consider what the nervous system is like. Nerves terminate at one end in a sense organ and at the other end ultimately in a muscle.

In Figure II, A is a sense organ, B a nerve going from the sense organ to the brain C. D, E, F, G, and H are motor nerves going from the brain to the muscles. Now, let us show from the diagram what organization means and what tendency means. At first when the child sees the expression "nine times nine," he does not say "eighty-one." The stimulus brings about no definite action. It is as likely to go out through E or F as through D. But suppose we can get the child to say "nine times nine equals eighty-one." We can write the expression on the blackboard and have the child look at it and say "nine times nine equals eighty-one." Suppose the act of saying "eighty-one" is brought about by the nerve-current going out through nerve-chain D. By repetition, we establish a bond. A stimulus of a particular kind comes through A, goes over B to C, and out over D, making muscles at M bring about a very definite action in saying "eighty-one."

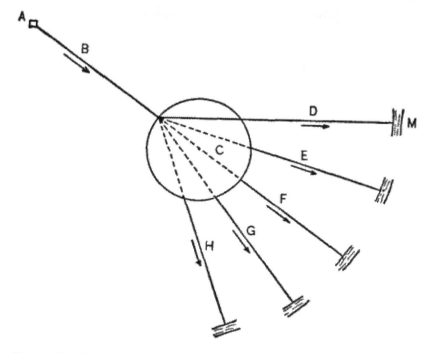

FIGURE II.—THE ORGANIZATION OF TENDENCIES

From the point of view of physiology, the process of habit-formation consists in securing a particular nerve coupling, establishing a particular nerve path, so that a definite form of stimulation will bring about a definite form of response. A nerve tendency is simply the likelihood that a stimulus will take a certain course rather than any other. This likelihood is brought about by getting the stimulus to take the desired route through the nervous system to a group of muscles and to continue following this route. The more times it passes the same way, the greater is the probability that at any given time the stimulus will take the accustomed route and bring about the usual response. At first any sort of action is possible. A nerve stimulus can take any one of the many routes to the different muscles. By chance or by conscious direction, the stimulus takes a certain path, and by repetition we fix and make permanent this particular route. This constitutes a nerve tendency or habit.

Plasticity. Our discussion should have made it clear that habit is acquired nature, while instinct is inherited nature. Habit is acquired tendency while instinct is inherited tendency. The possibility of acquiring habits is peculiarly a human characteristic. While inanimate things have a definite nature, a definite way of reacting to forces which act upon them, they have little, if any, possibility of varying their way of acting. Water might be said to have habits. If one cools water, it turns to ice. If we heat it, it turns to steam. But it *invariably* does this. We cannot teach it any different way of acting. Under the same conditions it always does the same thing.

Plants are very much like inanimate things. Plants have definite ways of acting. A vine turns around a support. A leaf turns its upper surface to the light. But one cannot teach plants different ways of acting. The lower forms of animals are somewhat like plants and inanimate objects. But to a very slight extent they are variable and can form habits. Among the higher animals, such as dogs and other domestic animals, there is a greater possibility of forming habits. In man there are the greatest possibilities of habit-formation. In man the learned acts or habits are many as compared to the unlearned acts or instincts; while among the lower animals the opposite is the case—their instincts are many as compared to their habits.

We may call this possibility of forming habits *plasticity*. Inanimate objects such as iron, rocks, sulphur, oxygen, etc., have no plasticity. Plants have very little possibility of forming habits. Lower animals have somewhat more, and higher animals still more, while man has the greatest possibility of forming habits. This great possibility of forming habits is one of the main characteristics of man. Let us illustrate the contrast between man and inanimate objects by an example. If sulphur is put into a test tube and heated, it at first melts and becomes quite thin like water. If it is heated still more, it becomes thick and will not run out of the tube. It also becomes dark. Sulphur *always* does this when so treated. It cannot be taught to act differently. Now the action of sulphur when heated is like the action of a man when he turns to the right upon meeting a person in the street. But the man has to acquire this habit, while the sulphur does not have to learn its way of acting. Sulphur always acted in this way, while man did not perform his act at first, but had to learn it by slow repetition. Everything in the world has its own peculiar nature, but man is unique in that his nature can be very much changed. To a large extent, a man is *made*, his nature is *acquired*. After we become men and women, we have hundreds and thousands of tendencies to action, definite forms of action, that we did not have when young. Man's nature might be said to consist in his tendencies to action. Some of these tendencies he inherits; these are his instincts. Some of these he acquires; these are his habits.

What Habits Do for Us. We have found out what habits are like; let us now see what they do for us. What good do they accomplish for us? How are we different after forming a habit from what we were before? We can best answer these questions by a consideration of concrete cases. Typewriting will serve very well the purpose of illustration. We shall give the result of an actual experiment in which ten university students took part. During their first half hour of practice, they wrote an average of 120 words. At the end of forty-five hours of practice, they were writing an average of 680 words in a half hour

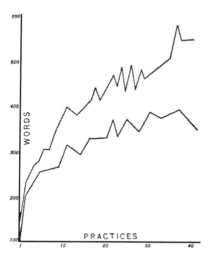

FIGURE III.—LEARNING CURVES

This was an increase of speed of 560 per cent. An expert typist can write about 3000 words in a half hour. Such a speed requires much more than forty-five hours practice, and is attained by the best operators only.

The upper graph shows the improvement in speed of a group of students working two half hours a day. The lower curve shows the improvement of a group working ten half-hours a day.

In the foregoing experiment, the students improved in accuracy also. At the beginning of the work, they made 115 errors in the half hour. At the end of the practice, with much faster speed, they were making only 327 errors in a half hour. The actual number of errors had increased 280 per cent. The increase in errors was therefore exactly half as much as the increase in speed. This, of course, was a considerable increase in accuracy, for while the speed had increased to 5.6 times what it had been at the beginning, the errors had increased only 2.8 times. The subjects in this experiment paid much more attention to speed than they did to accuracy. If they had emphasized accuracy, they would have been doing almost perfect work at the end of the practice, and their speed would have been somewhat less. Practice, then, not only develops speed but also develops accuracy.

There are also other results. At the beginning of work with the typewriter, there is much waste of energy and much fatigue. The waste of energy comes from using unnecessary muscles, and the fatigue is partly due to this waste of energy. But even apart from this waste of energy, an habituated act is performed with less fatigue. The various muscles concerned become better able to do their work. As a result of habituation there is, then, greater speed, greater accuracy, less waste of energy, and less fatigue.

If we look not at the changes in our work but at the changes in ourselves, the changes in our minds due to the formation of habits, we find still other results. At the beginning of practice with the typewriter, the learner's whole attention is occupied with the work. When one is learning to do a new trick, the attention cannot be divided. The whole mind must be devoted to the work. But after one has practiced for several weeks, one can operate the typewriter while thinking about something else. We say that the habituated act sinks to a lower level of consciousness, meaning that as a habit becomes more and more fixed, less and less attention is devoted to the acts concerned.

Increased skill gives us pleasure and also gives us confidence in our ability to do the thing. Corresponding to this inner confidence is outer certainty. There is greater objective certainty in our performance and a corresponding inner confidence. By objective certainty, we mean that a person watching our performance, becomes more and more sure of our ability to perform, and we ourselves feel confidence in our power of achievement.

Now that we have shown the results of habituation let us consider additional illustrations. In piano playing, the stimuli are the notes as written in the music. We see the notes occupying certain places on the scale of the music. A note in a certain place means that we must strike a certain key. At first the response is slow, we have to hunt out each note on the keyboard. Moreover, we make many mistakes; we strike the wrong keys just as we do in typewriting. We are awkward, making many unnecessary movements, and the work is tiresome and fatiguing. After long practice, the speed with which we can manipulate the keys in playing the piano is wonderful. Our playing becomes accurate, perfect. We do it with ease, with no unnecessary movements. We can play the piano, after we become skilled, without paying attention to the actual movements of our hands. We can play the piano while concentrating upon the meaning of the music, or while carrying on a conversation, or while thinking about something else. As a rule, pleasure and confidence come with skill. Playing a difficult piece on the piano involves a skill which is one of the most complicated that man achieves. It is possible only through habituation of the piano-playing movements.

Nailing shingles on a roof illustrates well the various aspects of habituation. The expert carpenter not only nails on many more shingles in a day than does the amateur, but he does it better and with more ease, and with much less fatigue. The carpenter knows exactly how much he can do in a day, and each particular movement is certain and sure. The carpenter has confidence in, and usually prides himself on, this ability, thus getting pleasure out of his work.

The operations in arithmetic illustrate most of the results of habituation. Practice in addition makes for speed and accuracy. In a few weeks' time we can very much increase our speed and accuracy in adding, or in the other arithmetical operations.

The foregoing examples are sufficient, although they could be multiplied indefinitely. Almost any habit one might name would show clearly most of the results enumerated. The most important aspects of habituation may be summed up in the one word *efficiency*. Habituation gives us speed and accuracy. Speed and accuracy mean skill. Skill means efficiency.

How Habits Are Formed. It is clear from the foregoing discussion that the essential thing in a habit is the definiteness of the connection between the stimulus and the response, between the situation and the reaction to the situation. Our question now is, how is this definiteness of connection established? The answer is, *through repetition*. Let us work the matter out from a concrete case, such as learning to play the piano. In piano playing the stimulus comes from the music as printed on the staff. A note having a certain position on the staff indicates that a certain key is to be struck. We are told by our music teacher what keys on the piano correspond to the various notes on the staff, or we may learn these facts from the instruction book. It makes no difference how we learn them; but after we know these facts, we must have practice to give us skill. The mere knowledge will not make us piano players. In order to be skillful, we must have much practice not only in striking the keys indicated by the various note positions, but with the various combinations of notes. For example, a note on the second space indicates that the player must strike the key known as "A." But "A" may occur with any of the other notes, it may precede them or it may follow them. We must therefore have practice in striking "A" in all these situations. To have skill at the piano, we must mechanize many performances. We must be able to read the notes with accuracy and ease. We must practice so much that the instant we see a certain combination of notes on the staff, our hands immediately execute the proper strokes. Not only must we learn what keys on the piano correspond to the various notes of the music, but the notes have a temporal value which we must learn. Some are to be sounded for a short time, others for a longer time. We have eighth notes, quarter notes, half notes, etc. Moreover, the signature of the music as indicated by the sharps or flats changes the whole situation. If the music is written in "A sharp" then when "A" is indicated on the staff, we must not strike the white key known as "A," but the black key just above, known as "A sharp."

Briefly, in piano playing, the stimulus comes from the characters printed on the staff. The movements which these characters direct are very complicated and require months and years of practice. We must emphasize the fact that practice alone gives facility, years of practice. But after these years of practice, one can play a piece of music at sight; that is, the first stimulus sets off perfectly a very complicated response. This sort of performance is one of the highest feats of skill that man accomplishes.

To get skill, then, one must practice. But mere repetition is not sufficient. For practice to be most effective, one must put his whole mind on what he is doing. If he divides his attention between the acts which he is practicing and something else, the effect of the practice in fixing and perfecting the habit is slight. It seems that when we are building up a new nerve-path which is to be the basis of a new habit, the nervous energies should not be divided; that the whole available nervous energy should be devoted to the acts which we are repeating. This is only another way of saying that when we are practicing to establish a habit, we should attend to what we are doing and to nothing else. But after the habit-connection is once firmly established, we can attend to other things while performing the habitual act. The habitual action will go on of itself. We may say, then, that in order to be able to do a thing with little or no attention, we must give much attention to it at first.

Another important factor in habit-formation is pleasure. The act which we are practicing must give us pleasure, either while we are doing it or as a result. Pleasurable results hasten habit-formation. When we practice an act in which we have no interest, we make slow progress or none at all. Now the elements of interest are attention and pleasure. If we voluntarily attend to a thing and its performance gives us pleasure, or pleasure results from it, we say we are interested in it. The secret of successful practice is interest. Repeatedly in laboratory experiments it happens that a student loses interest in the performance and subsequently makes little, if any, progress. One of the biggest problems connected with habit-formation is that of maintaining interest.

A factor which prevents the formation of habits is that of exceptions. If a stimulus, instead of going over to the appropriate response, produces some other action, there is an interference in the formation of the desired habit. The effect of an exception is greater than the mere neglect of practice. The *exception opens up another path* and tends to make future action uncertain. Particularly is this true in the case of moral habits. Forming moral habits is usually uphill work anyway, in that we have instincts to overcome. Allowing exceptions to enter, in the moral sphere, usually means a slipping back into an old way of acting, thereby weakening much the newly-made connection.

In any kind of practice, when we become fatigued we make errors. If we continue to practice when fatigued, we form connections which we do not wish to make and which interfere with the desired habits.

Economy of Practice. The principles which we have enumerated and illustrated are fairly general and of universal validity. There are certain other factors which we may discuss here under the head of economical procedure. To form a habit, we must practice. But how long should we practice at one time? This is an experimental problem and has been definitely solved. It has been proved by experiment that we can practice profitably for as long a time as we can maintain a high degree of attention, which is usually till we become fatigued. This time is not the same for all people. It varies with age, and in the case of the same person it varies at different times. If ordinary college students work at habit-formation at the highest point of concentration, they get the best return for a period of about a half hour. It depends somewhat on the amount of concentration required for the work and the stage of fixation of the habit, *i.e.* whether one has just begun to form the habit or whether it is pretty well fixed. For children, the period of successful practice is usually much less than a half hour—five, ten, fifteen, twenty minutes, depending upon the age of the child and the kind of work.

The best interval between periods of practice is the day, twenty-four hours. If one practices in the morning for a half hour, one can practice again in the afternoon with nearly as much return as he would secure the next day, but not quite. In general, practice is better, gives more return, if spread out. To practice one day as long as one can work at a high point of efficiency, and then to postpone further practice till the next day, gives one the most return for the time put in. But if one is in a hurry to form a habit, one can afford to practice more each day even if the returns from the practice do diminish proportionately.

This matter has been tried out on the typewriter. If one practices for ten half hours a day with half-hour rests between, one does not get so much return for his time as he would if he should spread it out at the rate of one or two half-hour practices a day. But by working ten half hours a day, one gets much more efficiency in the same number of days than if he should practice only one or two half hours a day. This point must not be misunderstood. We do not mean that one must not work at anything longer than a half hour a day. We mean that if one is forming a habit, his time counts for more in forming the habit if spread out at the rate of a half hour or an hour a day, than it does if put in at a faster rate. Therefore if one is in no hurry and can afford to spread out his time, he gets the best return by so doing, and the habit is more firmly fixed than if formed hurriedly. But if one is in a hurry, and has the time to devote to it, he can afford to concentrate his practice up to five hours or possibly more in a day, provided that rest intervals are interspersed between periods of practice.

There is one time in habit-formation when concentrated practice is most efficient. That is at the beginning. In a process as complicated as typewriting, so little impression is made at the beginning by a short period of practice that progress is but slight. On the first day, one should practice about four or five times to secure the best returns, a half hour each time.

What the Teacher Can Do. Now, let us see how the teacher can be of assistance to the pupil in habit-formation. The teacher should have a clear idea of the nature of the habit to be formed and should demonstrate the habit to the pupil. Suppose the habit is so simple a thing as long division. The teacher should explain each step in the process. She should go to the blackboard and actually solve a number of problems in long division, so that the pupils can see just how to do it. After this the pupils should go to the board and solve a problem themselves. The reason for this procedure is that it is most economical. If the children are left to get the method of doing long division from a book, they will not be able to do it readily and will make mistakes. A teacher can explain a process better than it can be explained in a book. By giving a full explanation and demonstration and then by requiring the children to work a few problems while she watches for mistakes, correcting them at once, the teacher secures economy of effort and time. The first step is to demonstrate the habit to the pupils; the second, to have them do the act, whatever it is, correcting their mistakes; the third, to require the pupils to practice till they have acquired skill. The teacher must make provision for practice.

What Parents Can Do. Parents can be of very great assistance to children who are forming habits.

(1) They can coöperate with the school, which is directing the child in the systematic formation of a great system of habits. The teacher should explain these habits to the parents so that they may know what the teacher is trying to do. Quite often the home and the school are working at cross purposes. The only way to prevent this is for them to work in the closest coöperation, with the fullest understanding of what is being undertaken for the child. Parents and teachers should often meet together and talk over the work of training the children of the community. Parents should have not merely a general understanding of the work of the school, but they should know the details undertaken. The school often assigns practice work to be done at home in reading, writing, arithmetic. Parents should always know of these assignments and should help the children get the necessary practice. They can do this by reminding the child of the work, by preparing a suitable place where the work may be done, and by securing quiet for the practice. Children like play and it is easy for them to forget their necessary work. Parents can be of the greatest service to childhood and youth by holding the children to their responsibilities and duties.

Few parents take any thought of whether their children are doing all possible for their school progress. Few of those who do, make definite plans and arrangements for the children to accomplish the necessary practice and study. This is the parent's duty and responsibility. Moreover, parents are likely to feel that children have no rights, and think nothing of calling on them in the midst of their work to do some errand. Now, children should work about the house and help their parents, but there should be a time for this and a separate time for study and practice on school work.

When a child sits down for serious practice on some work, his time should be sacred and inviolable. Instead of interfering with the child, the parents should do everything in their power to make this practice possible and efficient. In their relations with their children perhaps parents sin more in the matter of neglecting to plan for them than in any other way. They plan for everything else, but they let their children grow up, having taken no definite thought about helping them to form their life habits and to establish these habits by practice. When a child comes home from school, the mother should find out just what work is to be done before the next day and should plan the child's play and work in such a way as to include all necessary practice. If all parents would do this, the value to the work of the school and to the life of the child would be incalculable.

(2) Just as one of the main purposes of the teacher is to help the child gain initiative, so it is one of the greatest of the parents' duties. Parents must help the children to keep their purposes before them. Children forget, even when they wish to remember. Often, they do not want to remember. The parents' duty is to get the child to *want* to remember, and to help him to remember, whether he wants to or not. One of the main differences between childhood and maturity is that the child lives in the present, his purposes are all immediate ones. Habits always look forward, they are for future good and use. Mature people have learned to look forward and to plan for the future. They must, therefore, perform this function for the children. They must look forward and see what the child should learn to do, and then see that he learns to do it.

(3) Parents must help children to plan their lives in general and in detail; *i.e.* in the sense of determining the ideals and habits that will be necessary for those lives. The parents must do this with the help of the child. The child must not be a blind follower, but as the child's mind becomes mature enough, the parent must explain the matter of forming life habits, and must show the child that life is a structure that he himself is to build. Life will be what he makes it, and the time for forming character is during early years. The parent must not only tell the child this but must help him to realize the truth of it, must help him continually, consistently.

(4) Of course it is hardly necessary to say that the parent can help much, perhaps most, by example. The parent must not only tell the child what to do but must *show* him how it should be done.

(5) Parents can help in the ways mentioned above, but they can also help by coöperating among themselves in planning for the training of the children of the community. One parent cannot train his children independently of all the other people in the community. There must be a certain unity of ideals and aims. Therefore, not only is there need for coöperation between parents and teachers but among parents themselves. Although they coöperate in everything else, they seldom do in the training of their children. The people of a community should meet together occasionally to plan for this common work.

Importance of Habit in Education and Life. A man is the sum of his habits and ideals. He has language habits; he speaks German, or French, or English. He has writing habits, spelling habits, reading habits, arithmetic habits. He has political habits, religious habits. He has various social habits, habitual attitudes which he takes toward his fellows. He has moral habits—he is honest and truthful, or he is dishonest and untruthful. He always looks on the bright side, or else on the dark side of events. All these habits and many more, he has. They are structures which he has built. One's life, then, is the sum of his tendencies, and these tendencies one establishes in early life.

This view gives an importance to the work of the school which is derived from no other view. The school is not a place where we get this little bit of information, or the other. It is the place where we are molded, formed, and shaped into the beings we are to be. The school has not risen to see the real importance of its work. Its aims have been low and its achievements much lower than its aims. Teachers should rise to the importance of their calling. Their work is that of gods. They are creators. They do not make the child. They do not give it memory or attention or imagination. But they are creators of tendencies, prejudices, religions, politics, and other habits unnumbered. So that in a very real sense, the school, with all the other educational influences, makes the man. We do not give a child the capacity to learn, but we can determine what he shall learn. We do not give him memory, but we can select what he shall remember. We do not make the child as he is at the beginning, but we can, in large measure, determine the world of influences which complete the task of *making*.

In the early part of life every day and every hour of the day establishes and strengthens tendencies. Every year these tendencies become stronger. Every year after maturity, we resist change. By twenty-five or thirty, "character has set like plaster." The general attitude and view of the world which we have at maturity, we are to hold throughout life. Very few men fundamentally change after this. It takes a tremendous influence and an unusual situation to break one up and make him an essentially different man after maturity. Every year a "crank" becomes "crankier."

It is well that this is so. Everything in the world costs its price. Rigidity is the price we pay for efficiency. In order to be efficient, we must make habitual the necessary movements. After they are habituated, they resist change. But habit makes for regularity and order. We could not live in society unless there were regularity, order, fixity. Habit makes for conservatism. But conservatism is necessary for order. In a sense, habit works against progress. But permanent improvement without habit would be impossible, for permanent progress depends upon holding what we gain. It is well for society that we are conservative. We could not live in the chaos that would exist without habit. Public opinion resists change. People refuse to accept a view that is different from the one they have held. We could get nowhere if we continually changed, and it is well for us that we continue to do the old way to which we have become accustomed, till a new and better one is shown beyond doubt. Even then, it is probably better for an old person to continue to use the accustomed methods of a lifetime. Although better methods are developed, they will not be so good for the old person as those modes of action that he is used to. The possibility of progress is through new methods which come in with each succeeding generation.

When we become old we are not willing to change, but the more reasonable of us are willing that our children should be taught a better way. Sometimes, of course, we find people who say that what was good enough for them is good enough for their children. Most of us think better, and wish to give our children a "better bringing up than ours has been."

These considerations make clear the importance of habit in life. They should also make clear a very important corollary. If habits are important in life, then it is the duty of parents and teachers to make a careful selection of the habits that are to be formed by the children. The habits that will be necessary for the child to form in order to meet the various situa tions of his future life, should be determined. There should be no vagueness about it. Definite habits, social, moral, religious, intellectual, professional, etc., will be necessary for efficiency. We should know what these various habits are, and should then set about the work of establishing them with system and determination, just as we would the building of a house. Much school work and much home training is vague, indefinite, uncertain, done without a clear understanding of the needs or of the results. We therefore waste time, years of the child's life, and the results are unsatisfactory.

Drill in School Subjects. In many school subjects, the main object is to acquire skill in certain processes. As previously explained, we can become skillful in an act only by repetition of the act. Therefore, in those subjects in which the main object is the acquiring of skill, there must be much repetition. This repetition is called drill. The matter of economical procedure in drill has already been considered, but there are certain problems connected with drill that must be further discussed.

Drill is usually the hardest part of school work. It becomes monotonous and tiresome. Moreover, drill is always a means. It is the means by which we become efficient. Take writing, for example. It is not an end in itself; it is the means by which we convey thoughts. Reading is a means by which we are able to get the thought of another. In acquiring a foreign language, we have first to master the elementary tools that will enable us to make the thought of the foreign language our own.

It seems that the hardest part of education always comes first, when we are least able to do it. It used to be that nearly all the work of the school was drill. There was little school work that was interesting in itself. In revolt against this kind of school, many modern educators have tried to plan a curriculum that would be interesting to the child. In schools that follow this idea, there is little or no drill, pure and simple. There is no work that is done for the sole purpose of acquiring skill. The work is so planned that, in pursuing it, the child will of necessity have to perform the necessary acts and will thereby gain efficiency. In arithmetic, there is no adding, subtracting, multiplying, or dividing, only as such things must be done in the performance of something else that is interesting in itself. For example, the child plays store and must add up the sales. The child plays bean bag and must add up the score. Practice gained in this indirect way is known as incidental drill. Direct drill consists in making a direct approach; we wish to be efficient at adding, so we practice adding as such and not merely as incidental to something else.

This plan of incidental drill is in harmony with the principle of interest previously explained. There are several things, however, that must be considered. The proper procedure would seem to be to look forward and find out in what directions the child will need to acquire skill and then to help him acquire it in the most economical way and at the proper time. Nature has so made us that we like to do a new trick. When we have taught a child how to add and subtract, he likes to perform these operations because the operations themselves give pleasure. Therefore much repetition can be allowed and much skill acquired by a direct approach to the practice. When interest drags, incidental drill can be fallen back upon to help out the interest. Children should be taught that certain things must be done, certain skill must be acquired. They should accept some things on the authority of elders. They should be taught to apply themselves and to give their whole attention to a thing that must be done. A desire for efficiency can be developed in them. The spirit of competition can sometimes be effectively used to add interest to drill. Of course, interest and attention there must be, and if it cannot be secured in one way, it must be in another.

Experiments have abundantly shown the value of formal drill, that is to say, drill for drill's sake. If an arithmetic class is divided, one half being given a few minutes' drill on the fundamental operations each day but otherwise doing exactly the same work as the other half of the class, the half receiving the drill acquires much more skill in the fundamental operations and, besides, is better at reasoning out problems than the half that had no drill. The explanation of the latter fact is doubtless that the pupils receiving the drill acquire such efficiency in the fundamental operations that these cause no trouble, leaving all the energies of the pupils for reasoning out the problems.

It has been shown experimentally that a direct method of teaching spelling is more efficient than an indirect method. It is not to be wondered at that such turns out to be the case. For in a direct approach, the act that we are trying to habituate is brought more directly before consciousness, receiving that focal attention which is necessary for the most efficient practice in habit-formation. If one wishes to be a good ball pitcher, one begins to pitch balls, and continues pitching balls day after day, morning, noon, and night. One does not go about it indirectly. If one wishes to be a good shot with a rifle, one gets a rifle and goes to shooting. Similarly, if one wishes to be a good adder, the way to do is to begin adding, not to begin doing something else. Of course any method that will induce a child to realize that he ought to acquire a certain habit, is right and proper. We must do all we can to give a child a desire, an interest in the thing that he is trying to do. But there is no reason why the thing should not be faced directly.

Rules for Habit Formation. In the light of the various principles which we have discussed, what rules can be given to one forming habits? The evident answer is, to proceed in accordance with established principles. We may, however, bring the most important of these principles together in the form of rules which can serve as a guide and help to one forming habits.

(1) *Get initiative.* By this is meant that a person forming a habit should have some sustaining reason for doing it, some end that is being sought. This principle will be of very little use to young children, only to those old enough to appreciate reasons and ends. In arithmetic, for example, a child should be shown what can be accomplished if he possesses certain skill in addition, subtraction, and multiplication. It is not always possible for a young person to see why a certain habit should be formed. For the youngest children, the practice must be in the form of play. But when a child is old enough to think, to have ideals and purposes, reasons and explanations should be worked out.

(2) *Get practice.* If you are to have skill, you must practice. Practice regularly, practice hard while you are doing it. Throw your whole life into it, as if what you are doing is the most important thing in the world. Practice under good conditions. Do not think that just any kind of practice will do. Try to make conditions such that they will enable you to do your best work. Such conditions will not happen by chance. You must make them happen. You must make conditions favorable. You must seek opportunities to practice. You must realize that your life is in the making, that *you* are making it, that it is to a large extent composed of habits. These habits you are building. They are built only by practice. Get practice. When practicing, fulfill the psychological conditions. Work under the most favorable circumstances as to length of periods, intervals, etc.

(3) *Allow no exceptions.* You should fully realize the great influence of exceptions. When you start in to form a habit, allow nothing to turn you from your course. Whether the habit is some fundamental moral habit or the multiplication table, be consistent, do not vacillate. Nothing is so strong as consistent action, nothing so weak as doubtful, wavering, uncertain action. Have the persistence of a bull dog and the regularity of planetary motion.

Transfer of Training. Our problem now is to find out whether forming one habit helps one to form another. In some cases it does. The results of a recent experiment performed in the laboratory of educational psychology in the University of Missouri, will show what is meant. It was found that if a person practiced distributing cards into pigeon holes till great proficiency was attained, and then the numbering of the boxes or pigeon holes was changed, the person could learn the new numbering and gain proficiency in distributing the cards in the new way more quickly than was the case at first. Similarly, if one learns to run a typewriter with a certain form of keyboard, one can learn to operate a different keyboard much more quickly than was the case in learning the first keyboard.

It is probable that the explanation of this apparent transfer is that there are common elements in the two cases. Certain bonds established in the first habit are available in the second. In the case of distributing the cards, many such common elements can be made out. One gains facility in reading the numbering of the cards. The actual movement of the hand in getting to a particular box is the same whatever the number of the box. One acquires schemes of associating and locating the boxes, schemes that will work in both cases. But suppose that one spends fifteen days in distributing cards according to one scheme of numbering, and then changes the numbering and practices for fifteen days with the new numbering, at the end of the second fifteen days one has more skill than at the close of the first fifteen days. In fact, in five days one has as much skill in the new method as was acquired in fifteen days in the first method. However, and this is an important point, the speed in the new way is not so great as the speed acquired in thirty days using one method or one scheme all the time. Direct practice on the specific habit involved is always most efficient.

One should probably never learn one thing *just because* it will help him in learning something else, for that something else could be more economically learned by direct practice. Learning one language probably helps in learning another. A year spent in learning German will probably help in learning French. But two years spent in learning French will give more effi ciency in French than will be acquired by spending one year on German and then one year on French. If the only reason for a study is that it helps in learning something else, then this study should be left out of the curriculum. If the only reason for studying Latin, for example, is that it helps in studying English, or French, or helps in grammar, or gives one a larger vocabulary in English on account of a knowledge of the Latin roots, then the study of the language cannot be justified; for all of these results could be much more economically and better attained by a direct approach. Of course, if Latin has a justification in itself, then these by-products are not to be despised.

The truth seems to be that habits are very specific things. A definite stimulus goes over to a definite response. We must decide what habits we need to have established, and then by direct and economical practice establish these habits. It is true that in pursuing some studies, we acquire habits that are of much greater applicability in the affairs of life than can be obtained from other studies. When one has acquired the various adding habits, he has kinds of skill that will be of use in almost everything that is undertaken later. So also speaking habits, writing habits, spelling habits, moral habits, etc., are of universal applicability. Whenever one undertakes to do a thing that involves some habit already formed, that thing is more easily done by virtue of that habit. One could not very well learn to multiply one number by another, such as 8,675,489 by 439,857, without first learning to add.

This seems to be all there is to the idea of the transfer of training. One gets an act, or an idea, or an attitude, or a point of view that is available in a new thing, thereby making the new thing easier. The methods one would acquire in the study of zoölogy would be, many of them, directly applicable in the study of botany. But, just as truly, one can acquire habits in doing one thing that will be a direct hindrance in learning another thing. Knocking a baseball unfits one for knocking a tennis ball. The study of literature and philosophy probably unfits one for the study of an experimental science because the methods are so dissimilar, in some measure antagonistic.

Habit and Moral Training. By moral training, we mean that training which prepares one to live among his fellows. It is a training that prepares us to act in our relations with our fellow men in such a way as to bring happiness to our neighbors as well as to ourselves. Specifically, it is a training in honesty, truthfulness, sympathy, and industry. There are other factors of morality but these are the most important. It is evident at once that moral training is the most important of all training. This is, at any rate, the view taken by society; for if a man falls short in his relations with his fellows, he is punished. If the extent of his falling is very great, his liberty is entirely taken away from him. In some cases, he is put to death. Moral training, in addition to being the most important, is also the most difficult. What the public schools can do in this field is quite limited. The training which the child gets on the streets and at home almost overshadows it.

Nature of Moral Training. A good person is one who does the right social thing at the right time. The more completely and consistently one does this, the better one is. What kind of training can one receive that will give assurance of appropriate moral action? Two things can be done to give a child this assurance. The child can be led to form proper ideals of action and proper habits of action. By ideal of action, we mean that the child should know what the right action is, and have a desire to do it. Habits of action are acquired only through action. As has been pointed out in the preceding pages, continued action of a definite kind develops a tendency to this particular action. One's character is the sum of his tendencies to action. These tendencies can be developed only through practice, through repetition. Moral training, therefore, has the same basis as all other training, that is, in habits. The same procedure that we use in teaching the child the multiplication table is the one to use in developing honesty. In the case of the tables, we have the child say "fifty-six" for "eight times seven." We have him do this till he does it instantly, automatically. Honesty and truthfulness and the other moral virtues can be fixed in the same way.

Home and Moral Training. The home is the most important factor in moral training. This is largely because of the importance of early habits and attitudes. Obedience to parents and respect for authority, which in a large measure underlie all other moral training, must be secured and developed in the early years of childhood. The child does not start to school till about six years old. At this age much of the foundation of morality is laid. Unless the child learns strict obedience in the first two or three years of life, it is doubtful whether he will ever learn it aright. Without the habit of implicit obedience, it is difficult to establish any other good habit.

Parents should understand that training in morality consists, in large measure, in building up habits, and should go about it in a systematic way. As various situations arise in the early life of a child, the parents should obtain from him the appropriate responses. When the situations recur, the right responses should be again secured. Parents should continue to insist upon these responses till tendencies are formed for the right response to follow when the situation arises. After continued repetition, the response comes automatically. The good man or woman is the one who does the right thing as the situation presents itself, does it as a matter of course because it is his nature. He does not even think of doing the wrong thing.

One of the main factors in child training is consistency. The parent must inflexibly require the right action in the appropriate situation. Good habits will not be formed if parents insist on proper action one day but on the next day allow the child to do differently.

Parents must plan the habits which they wish their children to form and execute these plans systematically, exercising constant care. Parents, and children as well, would profit from reading the plan used by Franklin. Farseeing and clear-headed, Franklin saw that character is a structure which one builds, so he set about this building in a systematic way. For a certain length of time he practiced on one virtue, allowing no exceptions in this one virtue. When this aspect of his character had acquired strength, he added another virtue and then tried to keep perfect as to both.

The School and Moral Training. In this, as in all other forms of training, the school is supplementary to the home. The teacher should have well in mind the habits and ideals that the home has been trying to develop and should assist in strengthening the bonds. The school can do much in developing habits of kind ness and sympathy among the children. It can develop civic and social ideals and habits. Just how it can best do this is a question. Should moral ideals be impressed systematically and should habits be formed at the time these ideals are impressed, or should the different ideals be instilled and developed as occasion demands? This is an experimental problem, and that method should be followed which produces the best results. It is possible that one teacher may use one method best while a different teacher will have better success with another method.

More important than the question of a systematic or an incidental method is the question of making the matter vital when it is taken up. Nothing is more certain than that mere knowledge of right action will not insure right action. In a few hours one can teach a child, as matters of mere knowledge, what he should do in all the important situations of life; but this will not insure that he will henceforth do the right things.

There are only two ways by which we can obtain any assurance that right action will come. The first way is to secure right habits of response. We must build up tendencies to action. Tendencies depend upon previous action. The second way is to help the child to analyze moral situations and see what results will follow upon the different kinds of action. There can be developed in a child a desire to do that which will bring joy and happiness to others, rather than pain and sorrow. But this analysis of moral situations is not enough to insure right moral action; there must be practice in doing the right thing. The situation must go over to the right response to insure its going there the next time. The first thing in moral training is to develop habits. Then, as soon as the child is old enough he can strengthen his habits by a careful analysis of the problem why one should act one way rather than another. This adds motive; and motive gives strength and assurance.

SUMMARY. Habits are acquired tendencies to specific actions in definite situations. They are fixed through repetition. They give us speed, accuracy, and certainty, they save energy and prevent fatigue. They are performed with less attention and become pleasurable. The main purpose of education is to form the habits—moral, intellectual, vocational, cultural—necessary for life. Habits and ideals are the basis of our mature life and character. Moral training is essentially like other forms of training, habit being the basis.

CLASS EXERCISES

1.   Practice on the formation of some habit until considerable skill is acquired. Draw a learning curve similar to the one showing the increase in skill. A class experiment can be performed by the use of a substitution test. Take letters to represent the nine digits, then transcribe numbers into the letters as described .Keep a record of successive five-minute periods of practice till all have practiced an hour. This gives twelve practice periods for the construction of a learning curve. The individual experiments should be more difficult and cover a longer period. Suitable experiments for individual practice are: learning to operate a typewriter, pitching marbles into a hole, writing with the left hand, and mirror writing. The latter is performed by standing a mirror vertically on the table, placing the paper in front and writing in such a way that the letters have the proper form and appearance when seen in the mirror. The subject should not look at his hand but at its reflection in the mirror. A piece of cardboard can be supported just over the hand so that only the image of the hand in the mirror can be seen.

2.   A study of the interference of habit can be made as follows: Take eight small boxes and arrange them in a row. Number each box plainly. Do not number them consecutively, but as follows, 5, 7, 1, 8, 2, 3, 6, 4. Make eighty cards, ten of each number, and number them plainly. Practice distributing the cards into the boxes. Note

the time required for each distribution. Continue to distribute them till considerable skill is acquired. Then rearrange the order of the boxes and repeat the experiment. What do the results show?

3.   Does the above experiment show any transfer of training? Compare the time for each distribution in the second part of the experiment, *i.e.* after the rearrangement of the boxes, with the time for the corresponding distribution in the first part of the experiment. The question to be answered is: Are the results of the second part of the experiment better than they would have been if the first part had not been performed? State your results and conclusions and compare with the statements in the text.

4.   A study of the effects of spreading out learning periods can be made as follows: Divide the class into two equal divisions. Let one division practice on a substitution experiment as explained in Exercise 1, for five ten-minute periods of practice in immediate succession. Let the other division practice for five days, ten minutes a day. What do the results indicate? The divisions should be of equal ability. If the first ten-minute practice period shows the sections to be of unequal ability, this fact should be taken into account in making the comparisons. Test sheets can be prepared by the teacher, or they can be obtained from the Extension Division of the University of Missouri.

5.   An experiment similar to No. 4 can be performed by practicing adding or any other school exercise. Care must be taken to control the experiment and to eliminate disturbing factors.

6.   Try the card-distributing experiment with people of different ages, young children, old people, and various ages in between. What do you learn? Is it as easy for an old person to form a habit as it is for a young person? Why?

7.   If an old person has no old habits to interfere, can he form a new habit as readily as can a young person?

8.   Cite evidence from your own experience to prove that it is hard for an old person to break up old habits and form new ones which interfere with the old ones.

9.   Do you find that you are becoming "set in your ways?"

10.   What do we mean by saying that we are "plastic in early years"?

11.   Have you planned your life work? Are you establishing the habits that will be necessary in it?

12.   Is it an advantage or a disadvantage to choose one's profession or occupation early?

13.   Attention often interferes with the performance of a habitual act. Why is this?

14.   If a man removes his vest in the daytime, he is almost sure to wind his watch. On the other hand if he is up all night, he lets his watch run down. Why?

15.   Do you know of people who have radically changed their views late in life?

16.   Try to teach a dog or a cat a trick. What do you learn of importance about habit-formation?

17.   What branches taught in school involve the formation of habits that are useful throughout life?

18.   Make a list of the moral habits that should be formed in early years.

19.   Write an essay on *Habit and Life*.

20.   Make a complete outline of the chapter.

REFERENCES FOR CLASS READING

- COLVIN AND BAGLEY: *Human Behavior*, Chapters XI and XVII.

- PILLSBURY: *Essentials of Psychology*, pp. 48–59; also Chapter XV.

- PYLE: *The Outlines of Educational Psychology*, Chapters X, XI, and XII.

- ROWE: *Habit Formation*, Chapters V–XIII.

- TITCHENER: *A Beginner's Psychology*, p. 169, par. 37.

CHAPTER VII

MEMORY

Perceptions and Ideas. In a previous chapter, brief mention was made of the difference between perceptions and ideas. This distinction must now be enlarged upon and made clearer. Perceptions arise out of our sensory life. We see things when these things are before our eyes. We hear things when these things produce air vibrations which affect our ears. We smell things when tiny particles from them come into contact with a small patch of sensitive membrane in our noses. We taste substances when these substances are in our mouths. Now, this seeing, hearing, smelling, tasting, etc., is *perceiving*. We perceive a thing when the thing is actually at the time affecting some one or more of our sense organs. A perception, then, results from the stimulation of a sense organ. Perception is the process of perceiving, sensing, objects in the external world.

Ideas are our *seeming* to see, hear, smell, taste things when these things are not present to the senses. This morning I saw, had a *perception* of, a robin. To-night in my study, I have an *idea* of a robin. This morning the robin was present. Light reflected from it stimulated my eye. To-night, as I have an idea of the robin, it is not here; I only seem to see it. The scene which was mine this morning is now revived, reproduced. We may say, therefore, that ideas are the conscious representatives of objects which are not present to the senses. Ideas are revived experiences.

Revived experience is memory. Since it is memory that enables us to live our lives over again, brings the past up to the present, it is one of the most wonderful aspects of our natures. The importance of memory is at once apparent if we try to imagine what life would be without it. If our life were only perceptual, if it were only the sights and sounds and smells and tastes of the passing moment, it would have little meaning, it would be bare and empty. But instead of our perceptions being our whole life, they are only the starting points of life. Perceptions serve to arouse groups of memory images or ideas, and the groups of ideas enrich the passing moment and give meaning to the passing perceptions, which otherwise would have no meaning.

Suppose I am walking along the street and meet a friend. I see him, speak to him, and pass on. But after I have passed on, I have ideas. I think of seeing my friend the day before. I think of what he said and of what he was doing, of what I said and of what I was doing. Perhaps for many minutes there come ideas from my past experience. These ideas were aroused by the perception of my friend. The perception was momentary, but it started a long train of memory ideas.

I pass on down the street and go by a music store. Within the store, a victrola is playing *Jesus, Lover of My Soul.* The song starts another train of memory ideas. I think of the past, of my boyhood days and Sunday school, my early home and many scenes of my childhood. For several minutes I am so engrossed with the memory images that I scarcely notice anything along the street. Again, the momentary perception, this time of sounds, served to revive a great number of ideas, or memories, of the past.

These illustrations are typical of our life. Every moment we have perceptions. These perceptions arouse ideas of our past life and experience. One of these ideas evokes another, and so an endless chain of images passes along. The older we become, the richer is our ideational life. While we are children, the perceptions constitute the larger part of our mental life, but as we become older, larger and larger becomes the part played by our memory images or ideas. A child is not content to sit down and reflect, giving himself up to the flow of ideas that come up from his past experience, but a mature person can spend hours in recalling past experience. This means that the older we grow, the more we live in the past, the less we are bound down by the present, and when we are old, instead of perceptions being the main part of mental life, they but give the initial push to our thoughts which go on in an endless chain as long as we live.

The Physiological Basis of Memory. It will be remembered that the basis of perception is the agitation of the brain caused by the stimulation of a sense organ by an external thing or force. If there is no stimulation of a sense organ, there is no sensation, no perception. Now, just as the basis of sensation and perception is brain activity, so it is also the basis of ideas. In sensation, the brain activity is set up from without. In memory, when we have ideas, the brain activity is set up from within and is a fainter revival of the activity originally caused by the stimulation of the sense organ. Our ideas are just as truly condi tioned or caused by brain activity as are our sensations.

Memory presents many problems, and psychologists have been trying for many years to solve them. We shall now see what they have discovered and what is the practical significance of the facts.

Relation of Memory to Age and Sex. It is a common notion that memory is best when we are young, but such is not the case. Numerous experiments have shown that all aspects of memory improve with age. Some aspects of memory improve more than others, and they improve at different times and rates; but all aspects do improve. From the beginning of school age to about fourteen years of age the improvement of most aspects of memory is rapid.

If we pronounce a number of digits to a child of six, it can reproduce but few of them, a child of eight or ten can reproduce more, a child of twelve can reproduce still more, and an adult still more. If we read a sentence to children of different ages, we find that the older children can reproduce a longer sentence. If we read a short story to children of different ages, and then require them to reproduce the story in their own words, the older children reproduce more of the story than do the young children.

Girls excel boys in practically all the aspects of memory.

In rote memory, that is, memory for lists of unrelated words, there is not much difference; but the girls are somewhat better. However, in the ability to remember the ideas of a story, girls excel boys at every age. This superiority of girls over boys is not merely a matter of memory. A girl is superior to a boy of the same age in nearly every way. This is merely a fact of development. A girl develops faster than a boy, she reaches maturity more quickly, in mind as well as in body. Although a girl is lighter than a boy at birth, on the average she gains in weight faster and is heavier at twelve than a boy of the same age. She also gains faster in height, and for a few years in early adolescence is taller than a boy of the same age. Of course, boys catch up and finally become much taller and heavier than girls. Similarly, a girl's mind develops faster than the mind of a boy, as shown in memory and other mental functions.

The Improvement of Memory by Practice. All aspects of memory can be improved by practice, some aspects much, other aspects little. The memory span for digits, or letters, or words, or for objects cannot be much improved, but memory for ideas that are related, as the ideas of a story, can be considerably improved. In extensive experiments conducted in the author's laboratory, it was found that a person who at first required an hour to memorize the ideas in a certain amount of material, could, after a few months' practice, memorize the same amount in fifteen minutes. And in the latter case the ideas would be better remembered than they were at the beginning of the experiment. Not only could a given number of ideas be learned in less time, but they would be better retained when learned in the shorter time. If a person comes to us for advice as to how to improve his memory, what should we tell him? In order to answer the question, we must consider the factors of a good memory.

Factors of a Good Memory. (1) The first requirement is to get a good impression in the beginning. Memory is revived experience. The more vivid and intense the first experience, the more sure will be the later recall. So if we wish to remember an experience, we must experience it in the first place under the most favorable conditions.

The thing must be seen clearly, it must be understood, it must be in the focus of consciousness.

The best teaching is that which leads the child to get the clearest apprehension of what is taught. If we are teaching about some concrete thing, a plant, a machine, we should be sure that the child sees the essential points, should be sure that the main principles enter his consciousness. We should find out by questioning whether he really does clearly understand what we are trying to get him to understand. Often we think a pupil or student has forgotten, when the fact is that he never really knew the thing which we wished to have him remember.

The first requisite to memory, then, is to *know in the first place*. If we wish to remember knowledge, the knowledge must be seen in the clearest light, really *be* knowledge, at the outset. Few people ever really learn how to learn. They never see anything clearly, they never stick to a point till it is apprehended in all its relations and bearings; consequently they forget, largely because they never really knew in the fullest sense.

Most teaching is too abstract. The teacher uses words that have no meaning to the pupil. Too much teaching deals with things indirectly. We study *about* things instead of studying things. In geography, for example, we study about the earth, getting our information from a book. We read about land formations, river courses, erosion, etc., when instead we should study these objects and processes themselves. The first thing in memory, then, is clear apprehension, clear understanding, vivid and intense impression.

(2) The second thing necessary to memory is to repeat the experience. First we must get a clear impression, then we must repeat the experience if we would retain it. It is a mistake to believe that if we have once understood a thing, we will always thereafter remember it. We must think our experiences over again if we wish to fix them for permanent retention.

We must organize our experience. To organize experience means to think it over in its helpful relations. In memory, one idea arouses another. When we have one idea, what other idea will this arouse? It depends on what connections this idea has had in our minds in the past. It depends on the associations that it has, and associations depend on our thinking the ideas over together.

Teachers and parents should help children to think over their experiences in helpful, practical relations. Then in the future, when an idea comes to mind, it brings along with it other ideas that have these helpful, practical relations. We must not, then, merely repeat our experiences, but must repeat them in helpful connections or associations. In organizing our experience, we must systematize and classify our knowledge.

One of the chief differences in men is in the way they organize their knowledge. Most of us have experiences abundant enough, but we differ in the way we work over and organize these experiences. Organization not only enables us to remember our experience, but brings our experience back in the right connections.

The advice that should be given to a student is the following: Make sure that you understand. If the matter is a lesson in a book, go through it trying to get the main facts; then go through it again, trying to see the relation of all the facts. Then try to see the facts in relation to your wider experience. If it is a history lesson, think of the facts of the lesson in their relation to previous chapters. Think of the details in their bearing on wider and larger movements.

A teacher should always hold in mind the facts in regard to memory, and should make her teaching conform to them. She should carefully plan the presentation of a new topic so as to insure a clear initial impression. A new topic should be presented orally by the teacher, with abundant illustration and explanation. It cannot be made too concrete, it cannot be made too plain and simple.

Then after the teacher has introduced and made plain the new topic, the pupil reads and studies further. At the next recitation of the class, the first thing in order should be a discussion, on the part of the pupils. This will help the pupils to get the facts cleared up and will help the teacher to find out whether the pupils have the facts right.

The first part of the recitation should also be a time for questions. Everything should now be made clear, if there are any errors or misunderstandings on the pupil's part. Of course any procedure in a recitation should depend upon the nature of the material and to some extent on the stage of advancement of the pupil; but in general such a procedure as that just outlined will be most satisfactory and economical: first clear initial presentation by the teacher; then reading and study on the part of the pupil, and third, discussions on the following day.

Teachers should also endeavor to show students how to study to the best advantage. Pupils do not know how to study. They do not know what to look for, and do not know how to find it after they know what they are looking for. They should be shown. Of course, some of them learn without help how to study. But some never learn, and it would be a great saving of time to help all of them master the arts of study and memorizing.

A very important factor in connection with memory is the matter of meaning. If a person will try to memorize a list of nonsense words, he will find that it is much more difficult than to memorize words that have meaning. This is a significant fact. It means that as material approaches nonsense, it is difficult to memorize. Therefore we should always try to grasp the meaning of a thing, its significance. In science, let us always ask, what is the meaning of this fact? What bearing does it have on other facts? How does it affect the meaning of other facts?

Kinds of Memories. We should not speak of memory as if it were some sort of power like muscular strength. We should always speak of *memories*. Memories may be classified from several different points of view: A classification may be based on the kind of material, as memory for concrete things, the actual objects of experience, on the one hand, and memory for abstract material, such as names of things, their attributes and relations, on the other. Again, we can base a classification on the type of ideation to which the material appeals, as auditory memory, visual memory, motor memory. We can also base a classi fication on the principle of *meaning*. This principle of classification would give us at least three classes: memory for ideas as expressed in sentences, logical memory; memory for series of meaningful words not logically related in sentences, rote memory; memory for series of meaningless words, a form of rote memory. This classification is not meant to be complete, but only suggestive. With every change in the kind of material, the method of presenting the material to the subject, or the manner in which the subject deals with the material, there may be a change in the effectiveness of memory.

While these different kinds or aspects of memory may have some relation to one another, they are to some extent independent. One may have a good rote memory and a poor logical memory, or a poor rote memory and a good logical memory. That is to say, one may be very poor at remembering the exact words of a book, but be good at remembering the meaning, the ideas, of the book. One may be good at organizing meaningful material but poor at remembering mere words. On the other hand, these conditions may be reversed; one may remember the words but never get the meaning. It is of course possible that much of this difference is due to habit and experience, but some of the difference is beyond doubt due to original differences in the nervous system and brain. These differences should be determined in the case of all children. It is quite a common thing to find a feeble-minded person with a good rote memory, but such a person never has a good logical memory. One can have a good rote memory without understanding, one cannot have a good logical memory without understanding.

Let us now ask the question, why can one remember better words that are connected by logical relations than words that have no such connection? If we read to a person a list of twenty nonsense words, the person can remember only two or three; but if a list of twenty words connected in a sentence were read to a person, in most cases, all of them would be reproduced. The reason is that the words in the latter case are not new. We already know the words. They are already a part of our experience. We have had days, perhaps years, of experience with them. All that is now new about them is perhaps a slightly new relation.

Moreover, the twenty words may contain but one, or at most only a few, ideas, and in this case it is the ideas that we remember. The ideas hold the words together. If the twenty words contain a great number of ideas, then we cannot remember all of them from one reading. If I say, "I have a little boy who loves his father and mother very much, and this boy wishes to go to the river to catch some fish," one can easily remember all these words after one reading. But if I say, "The stomach in all the Salmonidæ is syphonal and at the pylorus are fifteen to two hundred comparatively large pyloric cœca"; although this sentence is shorter, one finds it more difficult to remember, and the main reason is that the words are not so familiar.

Memory and Thinking. What is the relation of memory to thinking and the other mental functions? One often hears a teacher say that she does not wish her pupils to depend on memory, but wishes them to reason things out. Such a statement shows a misunderstanding of the facts; for reasoning itself is only the recall of ideas in accordance with the laws of association. Without memory, there would be no reasoning, for the very material of thought is found to be the revived experiences which we call ideas, memories.

One of the first requisites of good thinking is a reliable memory. One must have facts to reason, and these facts must come to one in memory to be available for thought. If one wishes to become a great thinker in a certain field, he must gain experience in that field and organize that experience in such a way as to remember it and to recall it when it is wanted.

What one does deplore is memory for the mere words with no understanding of the meaning. In geometry, for example, a student sometimes commits to memory the words of a demonstration, with no understanding of the meaning. Of course, that is worse than useless. One should remember the meaning of the demonstration. If one has memorized the words only, he cannot solve an original problem in geometry. But if he has understood the meaning of the demonstration, then he recalls it, and is enabled to solve the problem. If one does not remember the various facts about the relationships in a triangle, he cannot solve a problem of the triangle until he has worked out and discovered the necessary facts. Then memory would make them available for the solution of the problem.

Memory and School Standing. That memory plays a large part in our life is evident; and, of course, it is an important factor in all school work. It matters not what we learn, if we do not remember it. The author has made extensive experiments to determine the relation that memory has to a child's progress in school.

The method used was to give logical memory tests to all the children in a school and then rank the chil dren in accordance with their abilities to reproduce the story used in the test. Then they were ranked according to their standing in their studies. A very high correlation was found. On the whole, the pupils standing highest in the memory tests were found to stand highest in their studies. It is true, of course, that they did not stand highest merely because they had good memories, but because they were not only better in memory, but were better in most other respects too. Pupils that are good in logical memory are usually good in other mental functions.

A test of logical memory is one of the best to give us an idea of the school standing of pupils. Not only is the retention of ideas of very great importance itself, but the acquiring of ideas, and the organizing of them in such a way as to remember them involves nearly all the mental functions. The one who remembers well ideas logically related, is the one who pays the closest attention, the one

118

who sees the significance, the one who organizes, the one who repeats, the one who turns things over in his mind. A logical memory test is therefore, to some extent, a test of attention, association, power of organization as well as of memory; in a word, it is a test of mental power.

Other things being equal, a person whose power of retention is good has a great advantage over his fellows who have poor ability to remember. Suppose we consider the learning of language. The pupil who can look up the meaning of a word just once and remember it has an advantage over the person who has to look up the meaning of the word several times before it is retained. So in any branch of study, the person who can acquire the facts in less time than another person, has the extra time for learning something else or for going over the same material and organizing it better. The scientist who remembers all the significant facts that he reads, and sees their bearing on his problems, has a great advantage over the person who does not remember so well.

Of course, there are certain dangers in having a good memory, just as there is danger in being brilliant generally. The quick learner is in danger of forming slovenly habits. A person who learns quickly is likely to form the habit of waiting till the last minute to study his lesson and then getting a superficial idea of it. The slow learner must form good habits of study to get on at all.

Teachers and parents should prevent the bright children from forming bad habits of study. The person who learns quickly and retains well should be taught to be thorough and to use the advantage that comes from repetition. The quick learner should not be satisfied with one attack on his lesson, but should study the lesson more than once, for even the brilliant learner cannot afford to neglect the advantages that come from repetition. A person with poor memory and only mediocre ability generally can make up very much by hard work and by work that takes advantage of all the laws of economical learning. But he can never compete successfully with the person who works as hard as he does and who has good powers of learning and retention.

The author has found that in a large class of a hundred or more, there is usually a person who has good memory along with good mental ability generally, and is also a hard worker. Such a person always does the best work in the class. A person with poor memory and poor mental powers generally cannot hope to com pete with a person of good memory, good mental powers generally, if that person is also a good worker.

Learning and Remembering. A popular fallacy is expressed in the saying "Easy come, easy go." The person who is the best learner is also the best in retaining what is learned, provided all other conditions are the same. This matter was determined in the following way: A logical memory test was given to all the children in a city school system. A story was read to the pupils and then reproduced by them in writing. The papers were corrected and graded and nothing more was said about the test for one month. Then at the same time in every room, the teachers said, "You remember the story I read to you some time ago and which I asked you to reproduce. Well, I wish to see how much of the story you still remember." The pupils were then required to write down all the story that they could recall.

It was found that, in general, the children who write the most when the story is first read to them, write the most after the lapse of a month, and the poorest ones at first are the poorest ones at the end of the month. Of course, the correspondence is not perfect, but in some cases, in some grades, it is almost so.

The significance of this experiment is very great. It means that the pupil who gets the most facts from a lesson will have the most facts at any later time. This is true, of course, only if other things are equal. If one pupil studies about the matter more, reflects upon it, repeats it in his mind, of course this person will remember more, other things being equal. But if neither reviews the matter, or if both do it to an equal extent, then the one who learns the most in the first place, remembers the most at a later time.

I have also tested the matter out in other ways. I have experimented with a group of men and women, by reading a passage of about a page in length, repeating the reading till the subject could reproduce all the facts. It was found that the person who acquired all the facts from the fewest readings remembered more of the facts later. It must be said that there is less difference between the subjects later than at first.

In the laboratory of Columbia University a similar experiment was performed, but in a somewhat different way. Students were required to commit to memory German vocabularies and were later tested for their retention of the words learned. It was found that those who learned the most words in a given time, also retained the largest percentage of what had been learned. It should not be surprising that this is the case. The quick learner is the one who makes the best use of all the factors of retention, the factors mentioned in the preceding paragraph—good attention, association, organization, etc.

Another experiment performed in the author's laboratory bears out the above conclusions. A group of students were required to commit to memory at one sitting a long list of nonsense syllables. The number of repetitions necessary to enable each student to reproduce them was noted. One day later, the students attempted to reproduce the syllables. Of course they could not, and they were then required to say them over again till they could just repeat them from memory. The number of repetitions was noted. The number of repetitions was much less than on the first day. On the third day, the process was repeated. The number of repetitions was fewer still. This relearning was kept up each day till each person could repeat the syllables from memory without any study. It was found that the person who learned the syllables in the fewest repetitions the first time, relearned them in the fewest repetitions on succeeding days. All the experiments bearing on the subject point to the same conclusion; namely, that the quick learner, if other things are equal, retains at least as well as the slow learner, and usually retains better.

Transfer of Memory Training. We have said above that there are many kinds or aspects of memory. It has also been said that we can improve memory by practice. Now, the question arises, if we improve one aspect of memory, does this improve all aspects? This is an important question; moreover, it is one to be settled by experiment and not by argument.

The most extensive and thorough experiment was performed by an English psychologist, Sleight. The experiment was essentially as follows: He took a large number of pupils and tested the efficiency of the various aspects of their memory. He then took half of them and trained one aspect of their memory until there was considerable improvement. The other section had no memory training meanwhile. After the training, both groups again had all aspects of their memory tested. Both groups showed improvement in all aspects because the first tests gave them some practice, but the group that had been receiving the training was no better in those aspects not trained than was the group receiving no training at all. Aspects of memory much like the one trained showed some improvement, but other aspects did not.

The conclusion is that memory training is specific, that it affects only the kind of memory trained, and related memories. This is in harmony with what we learned about habit. When we receive training, it affects only the parts of us trained and other closely related parts.

Learning by Wholes. We do not often have to commit to memory verbatim, but when we do, it is important that we should know the most economical way. Experiments have clearly demonstrated that the most economical way is to read the entire selection through from beginning to end and continue to read it through in this way till the matter is learned by heart.

In long selections, the saving by this method is considerable. A pupil is not likely to believe this because if he spends a few minutes learning in this manner, he finds that he cannot repeat a single line, while if he had concentrated on one line, he could have repeated at least that much. This is true; but although he cannot repeat a single line by the whole procedure, he has learned nevertheless. It would be a good thing to demonstrate this fact to a class; then the pupils would be satisfied to use the most economical procedure. The plan holds good whether the matter be prose or poetry.

But experiments have been carried on only with verbatim learning. The best procedure for learning the facts so that one can give them in one's own words has not yet been experimentally determined.

Cramming. An important practical question is whether it pays to go over a great amount of material in a very short time, as students often do before examinations. From all that has been said above, one could infer the solution to this problem. Learning and memorizing are to some extent a growth, and consequently involve time.

There is an important law of learning and memory known as Jost's law, which may be stated as follows: If we repeat or renew associations, the repetitions have most value for the old associations. Therefore when we learn, we should learn and then later relearn. This will make for permanent retention. Of course, if we wish to get together a great mass of facts for a temporary purpose and do not care to retain them permanently, cramming is the proper method. If we are required to pass an examination in which a knowledge of many details is expected and these details have no important permanent value, cramming is justified. When a lawyer is preparing a case to present to a court, the actual, detail evidence is of no permanent value, and cramming is justified.

But if we wish to acquire and organize facts for their permanent value, cramming is not the proper procedure. The proper procedure is for a student to go over his work faithfully as the term of school proceeds, then occasionally review. At the end of the term, a rapid review of the whole term's work is valuable. After one has studied over matter and once carefully worked it out, a quick view again of the whole subject is most valuable, and assists greatly in making the acquisition permanent. But if the matter has not been worked out before, the hasty view of the material of the course, while it may enable one to pass the examination, has no permanent value.

Function of the Teacher in Memory Work. The function of a teacher is plainly to get the pupils to learn in accordance with the laws of memory above set forth; but there are certain things that a teacher can do that may not have become evident to the reader. It has been learned in experiments in logical memory that when a story is read to a subject and the subject attempts to reproduce it, certain mistakes are made. When the story is read again, it is common for the same mistakes to be made in the recall. Certain ideas were apprehended in a certain way; and, when the piece is read again, the subject pays no more attention to the ideas already acquired and reported, and they are therefore reported wrongly as they were in the first place. Often the subject does not notice the errors till his attention is called to them.

This suggests an important function of the teacher in connection with the memory work of the pupils. This function is to correct mistakes in the early stages of learning. A teacher should always be on the watch to find the errors of the pupils and to correct them before they are fixed by repetition.

A teacher should, also, consider it her duty to test the memory capacities of the pupils and to give each the advice that the case demands.

Some Educational Inferences.—There are certain consequences to education that follow from the facts of memory above set forth that are of considerable significance. Many things have been taught to children on the assumption that they could learn them better in childhood than later, because it was thought that memory and the learning capacity were better in childhood. But both of these assumptions are false. As children grow older their learning capacity increases and their memories become better.

It has particularly been held that rote memory is better in childhood and that therefore children should begin their foreign language study early. It is true that as far as *speaking* a foreign language is concerned, the earlier a child begins it the better. But this is not true of learning to read the language. The sounds of the foreign language that we have not learned in childhood in speaking the mother tongue are usually difficult for us to make. The organs of speech become set in the way of their early exercise. In reading the foreign language, correct pronunciation is not important. We are concerned with *getting* the thought, and this is possible without pronouncing at all. Reference to graphs will show that rote memory steadily improves throughout childhood and youth. The author has performed numerous experiments to test this very point. He has had adults work side by side with children at building up new associations of the rote memory type and found that always the adult could learn faster than the child and retain better what was learned.

The experience of language teachers in college and university does not give much comfort to those who claim that language study should be begun early. These teachers claim that the students who have had previous language study do no better than those who have had none. It seems, however, that there certainly ought to be *some* advantage in beginning language study early and spreading the study out over the high school period. But what is gained does not offset the tremendous loss that follows from requiring *all* high school students to study a foreign language merely to give an opportunity for early study to those who are to go on in the university with language courses. A mature university student that has a real interest in language and literature can begin his language study in the university and make rapid progress. Some of the best classical scholars whom the author knows began their language study in the university. While it would have been of some advantage to them to have begun their language study earlier, there are so few who should go into this kind of work that society cannot afford to make provision for their beginning the study in the high school.

The selection and arrangement of the studies in the curriculum must be based on other grounds than the laws of memory. What children make most progress in and need most to know are the concrete things of their physical and social environment. Children must first learn the world—the woods and streams and birds and flowers and plants and animals, the earth, its rocks and soils and the wonderful forces at work in it. They must learn man,—what he is and what he does and how he does it; how he lives and does his work and how he governs himself. They should also learn to read and to write their mother tongue, and should learn something of that great store of literature written in the mother tongue.

The few that are to be scholars in language and literature must wait till beginning professional study before taking up their foreign language; just as a person who is to be a lawyer or physician must also wait till time to enter a university before beginning special professional preparation. The child's memory for abstract conceptions is particularly weak in early years; hence studies should be so arranged as to acquaint the child with the concrete aspects of the world first, and later to acquaint him with the abstract relations of things. Mathematics should come late in the child's life, for the same reason. Mathematics deals with quantitative relations which the child can neither learn nor remember profitably and economically till he is more mature. The child should first learn the world in its descriptive aspects.

Memory and Habit. The discussion up to this point should have made it clear to the reader that memory is much the same thing as habit. Memory considered as retention depends upon the permanence of the impression on the brain; but in its associative aspects depends on connections between brain centers, as is the case with habit. The association of ideas, which is the basis of their recall, is purely a matter of habit formation.

When I think of George Washington, I also think of the Revolution, of the government, of the presidency, of John Adams, Thomas Jefferson, etc., because of the connections which these ideas have had in my mind many times before. There is a basis in the brain structure for these connections. There is nothing in any *idea* that connects it with another idea. Ideas become connected because of the *way in which we experience them,* and the reason one idea calls up another idea is because the brain process that is the cause of one idea brings about another brain process that is the cause of a second idea. The whole thing is merely a matter of the way the brain activities become organized. Therefore the various laws of habit-formation have application to memory in so far as memory is a matter of the association of ideas, based on brain processes.

One often has the experience of trying to recall a name or a fact and finds that he cannot. Presently the name or fact may come, or it may not come till the next day or the next week. What is the cause of this peculiar phenomenon?

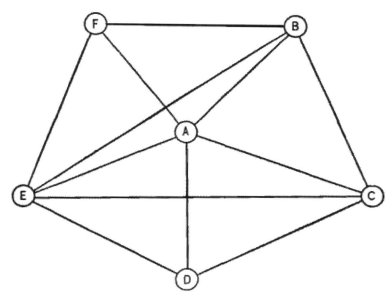

FIGURE IV—ASSOCIATIVE CONNECTIONS

The diagram represents schematically the neural basis of the association of ideas.

The explanation is to be found in the nervous system. When one tries to recall the name and it will not come to mind, there is some temporary block or hindrance in the nerve- path that leads from one center to the other and one cannot think of the name till the obstruction is removed. We go on thinking about other things, and in the meantime the activities going on in the brain remove the obstruction; so when the matter comes up again, the nerve current shoots through, and behold, the name comes to mind.

Now the only preventive of such an occurrence is to be found in the law of habit, for the block ordinarily occurs in case of paths or bonds not well established. We must *think together* the things we wish to have associated. Repetition is the key to the situation, repetition which is the significant thing in habit-formation, repetition which is the only way of coupling two things which we wish to have associated together.

Of course, there is no absolute coupling of two ideas. One sometimes forgets his own name. When we are tired or ill, things which were the most closely associated may not hang together. But those ideas hold together in the firmest way that have been experienced together most often in a state of attention. The diagram. illustrates schematically the neural connections and cross-connections which are the bases of the association of ideas, the circles *A, B, C, D, E,* and *F* represent brain processes which give rise to ideas, and the lines represent connecting paths. Note that there are both direct and indirect connections.

SUMMARY. Sensation and perception give us our first experience with things; memory is revived experience. It enables us to live our experience over again and is therefore one of the most important human traits. The physiological basis of memory is in the brain and nervous system. Memory improves with practice and up to a certain point with the age of the person. It is better in girls than in boys. Good memory depends on vivid experience in the first place and on organization and repetition afterward. The person who learns quickly usually retains well also. Memory training is specific.

The extension of the learning process over a long time is favorable to memory. Memory ideas are the basis of thinking and reasoning.

CLASS EXERCISES

1.   The teacher can test the auditory memory of the members of the class for rote material by using letters. It is better to omit the vowels, using only the consonants. Prepare five groups of letters with eight letters in a group. Read each group of letters to the class, slowly and distinctly. After reading a group, allow time for the students to write down what they recall, then read the next group and so proceed till the five groups have been read. Grade the work by finding the number of letters reproduced, taking no account of the position of the letters.

2.   In a similar way, test visual memory, using different combinations of letters. Write the letters plainly on five large squares of cardboard. Hold each list before the class for as long a time as it took to read a group in experiment No. 1.

3.   Test memory for words in a similar way. Use simple words of one syllable, making five lists with eight words in a list.

4.   Test memory for objects by fastening common objects on a large cardboard and holding the card before the class. Put eight objects on each card and prepare five cards. Expose them for the same length of time as in experiment No. 2.

5.   Test memory for *names* of objects by preparing five lists of names, eight names in a list, and reading the names as in experiment No. 1.

6.   You now have data for the following study: Find the average grade of each student in the different experiments. Find the combined grade of each student in all the above experiments. Do the members of the class hold the same rank in all the tests? How do the boys compare with the girls? How does memory for objects compare with memory for names of objects? How does auditory

memory compare with visual? What other points do you learn from the experiments?

7. The teacher can make a study of the logical memory of the members of the class by using material as described.Make five separate tests, using stories that are well within the comprehension of the class and that will arouse their interest. Sufficient material will be found in the author's *Examination of School Children* and Whipple's *Manual*. However, the teacher can prepare similar material.

8. Do the students maintain the same rank in the separate tests of experiment No. 7? Rank all the students for their combined standing in all the first five tests. Rank them for their combined standing in the logical memory tests. Compare the two rankings. What conclusions are warranted?

9. You have tested, in experiment No. 7, logical memory when the material was read to the students. It will now be interesting to compare the results of No. 7 with the results obtained by allowing the students to read the material of the test. For this purpose, select portions from the later chapters of this book. Allow just time enough for the selection to be read once slowly by the students, then have it reproduced as in the other logical memory experiment. Give several tests, if there is sufficient time. Find the average grade of each student, and compare the results with those obtained in No. 7. This will enable you to compare the relative standing of the members of the class, but will not enable you to compare the two ways of acquiring facts. For this purpose, the stories would have to be of equal difficulty. Let the members of the class plan an experiment that would be adequate for this purpose.

10. A brief study of the improvement of memory can be made by practicing a few minutes each day for a week or two, as time permits, using material that can be easily prepared, such as lists of common words. Let the members of the class plan the experiment. Use the best plan.

11.   The class can make a study of the relation of memory to school standing in one of the grades below the high school. Give at least two tests for logical memory. Give also the rote memory tests described.. Get the class standing of the pupils from the teacher. Make the comparison as suggested in Chapter I,. Or, the correlation can be worked out accurately by following the directions given in the *Examination of School Children*, page 58, or in Whipple's *Manual*, page 38.

12.   Let the members of the class make a plan for the improvement of their memory for the material studied in school. Plan devices for learning the material better and for fixing it in memory. At the end of the course in psychology, have an *experience*meeting and study the results reported.

13.   Prepare five lists of nonsense syllables, with eight in a list. Give them as in experiment No. 3, and compare the results with those of that experiment. What do the results indicate as to the value to memory of *meaningful* material? What educational inferences can you make? In preparing the syllables, put a vowel between two consonants, and use no syllable that is a real word.

14.   A study of the effects of distractions on learning and memory can be made as follows: Let the teacher select two paragraphs in later chapters of this book, of equal length and difficulty. Let the students read one under quiet conditions and the other while an electric bell is ringing in the room. Compare the reproductions in the two cases.

15.   From the chapter and from the results of all the memory tests, let the students enumerate the facts that have educational significance.

16.   Make a complete outline of the chapter.

REFERENCES FOR CLASS READING

*   COLVIN and BAGLEY: *Human Behavior*, Chapter XV.

- MÜNSTERBERG: *Psychology, General and Applied,* pp. 165–170.
- PILLSBURY: *Essentials of Psychology,* Chapters VI and VIII.
- PYLE: *The Outlines of Educational Psychology,* Chapter XIII.
- TITCHENER: *A Beginner's Psychology,* Chapter VII.

CHAPTER VIII

THINKING

In Chapter III we learned about sensation. We found that when a sense organ is stimulated by its appropriate type of stimulus, this stimulation travels through the sensory nerves and sets up an excitation in the brain. This excitation in the brain gives us sensation. We see if the eye is stimulated. We hear if the ear is stimulated, etc. In Chapter VII we learned that after the brain has had an excitation giving rise to sensation, it is capable of reviving this excitation later. This renewal or revival of a brain excitation gives us an experience resembling the original sensation, only usually fainter and less stable. This revived experience is called *image* or *idea*. The general process of retention and revival of experience is, as we have seen, known as memory. An idea, then, is a bit of revived experience. A perception is a bit of immediate or primary experience. I am said to perceive a chair if the chair is present before me, if the light reflected from the chair is actually exciting my retinas. I have an *idea* of the chair when I *seem* to see it, when the chair is not before me or when my eyes are shut. These distinctions were pointed out in the preceding chapter. Let us now proceed to carry our study of ideas further.

Association of Ideas. The subject of the association of ideas can best be introduced by an experiment. Take a paper and pencil, and think of the word "horse." Write this word down, and then write down other words that come to mind. Write them in the order in which they come to mind. Do this for three or four minutes, and try the experiment several times, beginning with a different word each time. Make a study of the lists of words. Compare the different lists and the lists written by different students.

In the case of the writer, the following words came to mind in the first few seconds: horse, bridle, saddle, tail, harness, buggy, whip, man, sky, stars, sun, ocean. Why did these words come, and why did they come in that order? Why did the idea "horse" suggest the idea "bridle"? And why did "bridle" suggest "saddle"? Is there something in the nature of ideas that couples them with certain other ideas and makes them *always* suggest the other ideas? No, there is not. Ideas become coupled together in our experience, and the coupling is in accordance with our experience. Things that are together in our experience become coupled together as ideas. The idea "horse" may become coupled with any other idea. The general law of the association of ideas is this: Ideas are joined together in memory or revived experience as they were joined in the original or perceptive experience.

But the matter is complicated by the fact that things are experienced in different connections in perceptive experience. I do not always experience "horse" together with "bridle." I sometimes see horses in a pasture eating clover. So, as far as this last experience is concerned, when I think "horse" I should also think "clover." I sometimes see a horse running when a train whistles, so "whistle" and "horse" should be coupled in my mind. A horse once kicked me on the shoulder, so "horse" and "shoulder" should be connected in my mind. And so they are. The very fact that these various experiences come back to me proves that they are connected in my mind in accordance with the original experiences. The revival of various horse experiences has come to me faster than I could write them down, and they are all bound together in my memory. If I should write them all out, it would take many hours, perhaps days.

Not only are these "horse ideas" bound together with one another, but they are bound more or less directly, more or less closely, to everything else in my life. I can, therefore, pass in thought from the idea "horse" to any other idea, directly or indirectly. Now, in any given case, what idea will actually come first after I have the idea "horse"? This depends upon the tendencies established in the nervous system. The brain process underlying the idea "horse" has connections with many other processes and tends to excite these processes. The factors that strengthen these tendencies or connections are the frequency, recency, primacy, and vividness of experience. Let us consider, in some detail, each of these factors.

Primacy of Experience. A strong factor in determining association is the *first experience*. The first, the original, coupling of ideas tends to persist. The first connection is nearly always a strong one, and is also strengthened by frequent repetition in memory. Our first experience with people and things persists with great strength, across the years, in spite of other associations and connections established later. Just now there comes to mind my first experience with a certain famous scientist. It was many years ago. I was a student in an eastern university. This man gave a public lecture at the opening of the session. I remember many details of the occurrence with great vividness. Although I studied under this man for three years, no other experience with him is more prominent than the first. First experiences give rise to such strong connections between ideas that these connections often persist and hold their own as against other connections depending upon other factors.

The practical consequences of this factor in teaching are, of course, evident. Both teachers and parents should take great care in the matter of the first experiences of children. If the idea-connections of first experiences are likely to persist, then these connections should be desirable ones. They should not be useless connections, nor should they, ordinarily, be connections that will have to be radically undone later. Usually it is not economical to build up connections between ideas that will not serve permanently, except in cases in which the immaturity of the mind makes such a procedure necessary.

Recency of Experience. The most recent connection of ideas is relatively strong, and is often the determining one. But the most recent connection must be very recent or it has no especial value. If I have seen a certain friend to-day, and his name is brought to mind now, to-day's experience with him will likely be brought to mind *first*. But if my last seeing him was some days or months ago, the idea-connection of the last meeting has no great value. Of course, circumstances always alter the matter. Perhaps we should say in the last instance that, other things being equal, the last experience has no special value. If the last experience was an unusual one, such as a death or a marriage, then it has a value due to its vividness and intensity and its emotional aspects. These factors not only add strength to the connections made at the time but are the cause of frequent revivals of this last experience in memory in the succeeding days. All these factors taken together often give a last experience great associative strength, even though the last experience is not recent.

Frequency of Experience. The most frequent connection of ideas is probably the most important factor of all in determining future associations. The first connection is but one, and the last connection is but one, while repeated connections may be many in number. Connections which recur frequently usually overcome all other connections. Hence frequency is the dominant factor in association. Most of the strength of first connections is due to repetitions in memory later. The first experience passes through the mind again and again as memory, and thereby becomes strengthened. The fact that repetition of connections establishes these connections is, of course, the justification of drill and review in school studies. The practical needs of life demand that certain ideas be associated so that one calls up the other. Teachers and parents, knowing these desirable connections, endeavor to fix them in the minds of children by repetition. The important facts of history, literature, civics, and science we endeavor, by means of repetition, to fasten in the child's mind.

Vividness and Intensity of Experience. A vivid experience is one that excites and arouses us, strongly stimulating our feelings. Such experiences establish strong bonds of connection. When I think of a railroad wreck, I think of one in which I participated. The experience was vivid, intense, and aroused my emotions. I hardly knew whether I was dead or alive. Then, secondly, I usually think of a wreck which I witnessed in childhood. A train plunged through a bridge and eighteen cars were piled up in the ravine. The experience was vivid and produced a deep and lasting impression on me.

The practical significance of this factor is, of course, great. When ideas are presented to pupils these ideas should be made clear. Every conceivable device should be used to clarify and explain,—concrete demonstration, the use of objects and diagrams, pictures and drawings, and abundant oral illustration. We must be sure that the one taught understands, that the ideas become focal in consciousness and take hold of the individual. This is the main factor in what is known as "interest." An interesting thing is one that takes hold of us and possesses us so that we cannot get away from it. Such experiences are vivid and have rich emotional connections or accompaniments. Ideas that are experienced together at such times are strongly connected.

Mental Set or Attitude. Another influence always operative in determining the association of ideas is mental set. By mental set we mean the mood or attitude one is in,—whether one is sad or glad, well or ill, fresh or fatigued, etc. What one has just been thinking about, what one has just been doing, are always factors that determine the direction of association. One often notices the effects of mental set in reading newspapers. If one's mind has been deeply occupied with some subject and one then starts to read a newspaper, one may actually miscall many of the words in the article he is reading; the words are made to fit in with what is in his mind. For example, if one is all wrought up over a wedding, many words beginning with "w" and having about the same length as the word "wedding," will be read as "wedding."

Mental set may be permanent or temporary. By permanent we mean the strong tendencies that are built up by continued thought in a certain direction. One becomes a Methodist, a Democrat, a conservative, a radical, a pessimist, an optimist, etc., by continuity of similar experiences and similar reactions to these experiences. Germans, French, Irish, Italians, Chinese, have characteristic sets or ways of reacting to typical situations that may be called racial. These prejudicial ways of reacting may be called racial sets or attitudes. Religious, political, and social prejudices may all be called sets or attitudes.

Temporary sets or attitudes are leanings and prejudices that are due to temporary states of mind. The fact that one has headache, or indigestion, or is in a hurry, or is angry, or is hungry, or is emotionally excited over something will, for the time, be a factor in determining the direction of association.

One of the tasks of education is to build up sets or attitudes, permanent prejudices, to be constant factors in guiding association and, consequently, action. We wish to build up permanent attitudes toward truth, honesty, industry, sympathy, zeal, persistence, etc. It is evident that attitude is merely an aspect of habit. It is an habitual way of reacting to a definite and typical situation. This habitual way is strengthened by repetition, so that set or attitude finally, after years of repetition, becomes a part of our nature. Our prejudices become as strong, seemingly, as our instinctive tendencies. After a man has thought in a particular groove for years, it is about as sure that he will come to certain definite conclusions on matters in the line of his thought as that he would give typical instinctive or even reflex reactions. We know the direction association will take for a Presbyterian in religious matters, for a Democrat in political matters, with about as much certainty as we know what their actions will be in situations that evoke instinctive reactions.

Thinking and Reasoning. Thinking is the passing of ideas in the mind. This flow of ideas is in accordance with the laws of association above discussed. The order in which the ideas come is the order fixed by experience, the order as determined by the various factors above enumerated.

In early life, one's mind is chiefly perceptual, it is what we see and hear and taste and smell. As one grows older his mind grows more and more ideational. With increasing age, a larger and larger percentage of our mental life is made up of ideas, of memories. The child lives in the present, in a world of perceptions. A man is not so much tied down to the present; he lives in memory and anticipation. He thinks more than does the child. A man is content to sit down in his chair and think for hours at a time, a child is not. This thinking is the passing of ideas, now one, then another and another. These ideas are the survivals or revivals of our past experience. The order of their coming depends on our past experience.

As I sit here and write, there surge up out of my past, ideas of creeks and rivers and hills, horses and cows and dogs, boys and girls, men and women, work and play, school days, friends,—an endless chain of ideas. This "flow" of ideas is often started by a perception. For illustration, I see a letter on the table, a letter from my brother. I then have a visual image of my brother. I think of him as I saw him last. I think of what he said. I think of his children, of his home, of his boyhood, and our early life together. Then I think of our mother and the old home, and so on and on. Presently I glance at a history among my books, and immediately think of Greece and Athens and the Acropolis, Plato, Aristotle, and Socrates, schoolmates and teachers, and friends connected in one way or another with my college study of Greek.

In this description of the process of thinking, I have repeatedly used the words "think of." I might have said instead, "there came to mind ideas of Athens, ideas of friends," etc. Thinking, then, is a general term for our idea-life.

Reasoning is a form of thinking. Reasoning, too, is a flow of ideas. But while reasoning is thinking, it is a special form of thinking; it is thinking to a purpose. In thinking as above described and illustrated, no immediate ends of the person are served; while in reasoning some end is always sought. In reasoning, the flow of ideas must reach some particular idea that will serve the need of the moment, the need of the problem at hand. Reasoning, then, is controlled thinking, thinking centering about a problem, about a situation that one must meet.

The statement that reasoning is *controlled* thinking needs some explanation, for the reader at once is likely to want to know what does the controlling. There is not some special faculty or power that does the controlling. The control is exercised by the set into which one is thrown by the situation which confronts one. The set puts certain nerve-tracts into readiness to conduct, or in other words, makes certain groups of ideas come into mind, and makes one satisfied only if the right ideas come. As long as ideas come that do not satisfy, the flow keeps on, taking one direction and then another, in accordance with the way our ideas have become organized. An idea finally comes that satisfies. We are then said to have reached a conclusion, to have made up our mind, to have solved our problem.

But the fact that we are satisfied is no sure sign that the problem is correctly solved. It means only that our past experiences, available at the time through association, say that the conclusion is right. Or, in more scientific terms, that the conclusion is in harmony with our past experience, as it has been organized and made available through association. There is not within us a little being, a reasoner, that sits and watches ideas file by and passes judgment upon them. The real judge is our nervous system with its organized bonds or connections.

An illustration may make the matter clearer: A boy walking along in the woods comes to a stream too wide for him to jump across. He wishes to be on the other side, so here is a situation that must be met, a problem that must be solved. A flow of ideas is started centering about the problem. The flow is entirely determined and directed by past experience and the present situation. The boy pauses, looks about, and sees on the bank a pole and several large stones. He has walked on poles and on fences, he therefore sees himself putting the pole across the stream and walking on it. This may be in actual visual imagery, or it may be in words. He may merely say, "I will put the pole across and walk on it." But, before having time to do it, he may recall walking on poles that turned. He is not then satisfied with the pole idea. The perception of stones may next become clear in his mind, and if no inhibiting or hindering idea comes up, the stone idea carries him into action. He piles the stones into the stream and walks across.

As was mentioned above, the flow of ideas may take different forms. The imagery may take any form but is usually visual, auditory, motor, or verbal.

Further discussion of the point that reasoning is determined by past experience may be necessary. Suppose the teacher ask the class a number of different questions, moral, religious, political. Many different answers to the questions will be received, in some cases as many answers to the questions as there are pupils. Ask whether it is ever right to steal, whether it is ever right to lie, whether it is ever right to fight, whether it is ever right to disobey a parent or teacher, whether oak is stronger than maple, whether iron expands more when heated than does copper, whether one should always feed beggars, etc. The answers received, in each case, depend on the previous experience of the pupils. The more nearly alike the experiences of the pupils, the more nearly alike will be the answers. The more divergent the experiences, the more different will be the answers.

The basis of reasoning is ultimately the same sort of thing as the basis of habit. We have repeated experiences of the same kind. The ideas of these experiences become welded together in a definite way. Association between certain groups of ideas becomes well fixed. Later situations involving these groups of ideas set up definite trains of association. We come always to definite conclusions from the same situations provided that we are in the same mental set and the factors involved are the same.

Throughout early life we have definite moral and religious ideas presented to us. We come to think in definite ways about them or with them. It therefore comes about that every day we live, we are determining the way we shall in the future reason about things. We are each day getting the material for the solution of the problems that will be presented to us by future situations. And the reason that one of us will solve those problems in a different way from another is because of having somewhat different experiences, and of organizing them in a different way.

Meaning and the Organization of Ideas. In the preceding paragraphs we have several times spoken of the organization of ideas. Let us now see just what is meant by this expression. Intimately connected with the organization of ideas is *meaning*. What is the meaning of an idea? The meaning of an idea is another idea or group of ideas that are very closely associated with it. When there comes to mind an idea that has arisen out of repeated experience, there come almost immediately with it other ideas, perhaps vivid images which have been connected with the same experience. Suppose the idea is of a horse. If one were asked, "What is a horse?" ideas of a horse in familiar situations would present themselves. One may see in imagination a horse being driven, ridden, etc., and he would then answer, "Why, a horse is to ride," or "A horse is to drive," or "A horse is a domestic animal," etc.

Again, "What is a cloud? What is the sun? What is a river? What is justice? What is love?" One says, "A cloud is that from which rain falls," or "A cloud is partially condensed vapor. The sun is a round thing in the sky that shines by day. A river is water flowing along in a low place through the land. Justice is giving to people what they deserve. Love is that feeling one has for a person which makes him be kind to that person." The answer that one gives depends on age and experience.

But it is evident that when a person is asked what a thing is or what is the meaning of a thing, he has at once ideas that have been most closely associated with the idea in question. Now, since the most important aspect of a thing is what we can do with it, what use it can be to us, usually meaning centers about *use*. A chair is to sit in, bread is to eat, water is to drink, clothes are to wear, a hat is a thing to be worn on one's head, a shovel is to dig with, a car is to ride in, etc.

Use is not quite so evident in such cases as the following: "Who was Cæsar? Who was Homer? Who is Edison? What was the Inquisition? What were the Crusades?" However, one has, in these cases, very closely associated ideas, and these ideas do center about what we have done with these men and events in our thinking. "Cæsar was a warrior. Homer was a writer of epics. Edison is an inventor," etc. These men and events have been presented to us in various situations as standing for various things in the history of the world. And when we think of them, we at once think of what they did, the place they fill in the world. This constitutes their meaning.

It is evident that an idea may have many meanings. And the meaning that may come to us at any particular moment depends upon the situation. A chair, for example, in one situation, may come to mind as a thing to sit in; in another situation, as a thing to stand in the corner and look pretty; in another, a thing to stand on so that one may reach the top shelf in the pantry; in another, a thing to strike a burglar with; in another, a thing to knock to pieces to be used to make a fire.

The meaning of a thing comes from our experience with it, and the thing usually comes to have more and more meanings as our experience with it increases. When we meet something new, it may have practically no meaning. Suppose we find a new plant in the woods. It has little meaning. We may be able to say only that it is a plant, or it is a small plant. We touch it and it pricks us, and it at once has more meaning. It is a plant that pricks. We bite into it and find it bitter. It is then a plant that is bitter, etc. In such a way, objects come to have meaning. They acquire meaning according to the connections in which we experience them and they may take on different meanings for different persons because of the different experiences of these persons. The chief interest we have in objects is in what use we can make of them, how we can make them serve our purposes, how we can make them contribute to our pleasure.

The organization of experience is the connecting, through the process of association, of the ideas that arise out of our experience.

Our ideas are organized not only in accordance with the way we experience them in the first place, but in accordance with the way we think them later in memory. Of course, ideas are recalled in accordance with the way we experience them, but since they are experienced in such a multitude of connections, they are recalled later in these various connections and it is possible in recall to repeat one connection to the exclusion of others.

Organization can therefore be a selective process. Although "horse" is experienced in a great variety of situations or connections, for our purposes we can select some one or more of these connections and by repetition in recalling it, strengthen these connections to the exclusion of others. Herein lies one of the greatest possibilities in thinking and reasoning, which enables us, to an extent, to be independent of original experience. We must have had experience, of course, but the strength of bonds between ideas need not depend upon original experience, but rather upon the way in which these ideas are recalled later, and especially upon the number of times they are recalled.

It is in the matter of the organization of experience that teachers and parents can be of great help to young people. Children do not know what connections of ideas will be most useful in the future. People who have had more experience know better and can, by direction and suggestion, lead the young to form, and strengthen by repetition, those connections of ideas that will be most useful later.

In the various school studies, a mass of ideas is presented. These ideas, isolated or with random connections, will be of little service to the pupils. They must be organized with reference to future use. This organization must come about through thinking over these ideas in helpful connections. The teacher knows best what these helpful connections are and must help the pupil to make them.

Suppose the topic studied in history is the Battle of Bunker Hill. The teacher should assist the child to think the battle over in many different connections. There are various geographical, historical, and literary aspects of the battle that are of importance. These aspects should be brought to mind and related by being thought of together. Thinking things together binds them together as ideas; and later when one idea comes, the others that have been joined with it in the past in thought, come also. Therefore, in studying the Battle of Bunker Hill, the pupil not only reads about it, but gets a map and studies the geography of it, works out the causes that led up to the battle, studies the consequences that followed, reads speeches and poems that have been made and written since concerning the battle, the monument, etc.

Similarly, all the topics studied in school should be thought over and organized with reference to meaning and with reference to future use. As a result of such procedure, all the topics become organized and crystallized, with all related ideas closely bound together in association.

One of the greatest differences in people is in the organization of their ideas. Of course, people differ in original experience, but they differ more in the way they organize this experience and prepare it for future needs. Just as in habit-formation we should by exercise and practice acquire those kinds of skill that will serve us best in the future, so in getting knowledge we should by repetition strengthen the connections between those ideas that we shall need to have connected in the future. All education looks forward and is preparatory. As a result of training in the organization of ideas, a pupil can learn how to organize his experience, in a measure, independent of the teacher. He learns to know, himself, what ideas are significant, and what connections of ideas will be most helpful. Such an outcome should be one of the ends of school training.

Training in Reasoning. We have already mentioned ways in which a child can be helped in gaining power and facility in reasoning. In this paragraph we shall discuss the matter more fully. There are three aspects of training in reasoning, one with reference to original experience, one with reference to the organization of this experience as just discussed, and one with reference to certain habits of procedure in the recall and use of experience.

(1) *Original experience.* Before reasoning in any field, one must have experience in that field. There is no substitute for experience. After having the experience, it can be organized in various ways, but experience there must be. Experience may be primary, with things themselves, or it may be secondary, received second hand through books or through spoken language. We cannot think without ideas, and ideas come only through perceptions of one kind or another.

Originally, all experience arises out of sensations. Language makes it possible for us to profit through the perceptual experience of others. But even when we receive our experience second hand, our own primary experience must enable us to understand the meaning of what we read and hear about, else it is valueless to us. Therefore, if we wish to be able to reason in the field of physics, of botany, of chemistry, of medicine, of law, or of agriculture, we must get experience in those fields. The raw material of thought comes only through experience. In such a subject as physical geography, for example, the words of the book have little meaning unless the child has had original experience in the matter discussed. He must have seen hills and valleys and rivers and lakes and rocks and weathering, and all the various processes discussed in physical geography; otherwise, the reading of the text is almost valueless. The same thing is true of all subjects. To reason in any subject we must have had original experience in it.

(2) *The organization of experience.* After experience comes its organization. This point has already been fully explained. It was pointed out that organization consists in thinking our experience over again in helpful relations. Here parents and teachers can be of very great service to children.

(3) *Habits of thought.* There are certain habits of procedure in reasoning, apart from the association of the ideas. One can form the habit of putting certain questions to oneself when a problem is presented, so that certain types of relations are called up. If one is a scientist, one looks for causes. If one is a lawyer, one looks up the court decisions. If one is a physician, one looks for symptoms, etc.

One of the most important habits in connection with reasoning is the habit of caution. Reasoning is waiting, waiting for ideas to come that will be adequate for the situation. One must form the habit of waiting a reasonable length of time for associations to run their course. If one act too soon, before his organized experience has had time to pass in review, he may act improperly. Therefore one must be trained to a proper degree of caution. Of course, caution may be overdone. One must act sometime, one cannot wait always.

Another habit is that of testing out a conclusion before it is finally put into practice. It is often possible to put a conclusion to some sort of test before it is put to the real test, just as one makes a model and tries out an invention on a small scale. One should not have full confidence in a conclusion that is the result of reasoning, till the conclusion has been put to the final test of experiment, of trial.

This last statement leads us to the real function of reasoning. Reason points the way to action in a new situation. After the situation is repeated for a sufficient number of times, action passes into the realm of habit.

Language and Thinking. The fact that man has spoken and written language is of the greatest significance. It has already been pointed out that language is a means through which we can get experience secondhand. This proves to be a great advantage to man. But language gives us still another advantage. Without language, thinking is limited to the passing of sensory images that arise in accordance with the laws of association. But man can name things and the attributes of things, and these names become associated, so that thinking comes to be, in part at least, a matter of words. Thinking is talking to oneself. One cannot talk without language.

The importance that attaches to language can hardly be overestimated. When the child acquires the use of language, he has acquired the use of a tool, the importance of which to thinking is greater than that of any other tool. Now, one can think without language, in the sense that memory images come and go,—we have defined thinking as the flow of imagery, the passing or succession of ideas. But after we have named things, thinking, particularly reasoning, becomes largely verbal, or as we said above,*talking to oneself.*

Not only do we give names to concrete things but we give names to specific attributes and to relations. As we organize and analyze our experiences, there appear uniformities, principles, laws. To these we give names, such as white, black, red, weight, length, thickness, justice, truth, sin, crime, heat, cold, mortal, immortal, evolution, disintegration, love, hate, envy, jealousy, possible, impossible, probable, etc. We spoke above of meanings. To meanings we give names, so that a single word comes to stand for meanings broad and significant, the result of much experience. Such words as "evolution" and "gravitation," single words though they are, represent a wide range of experiences and bring these experiences together and crystallize them into a single expression, which we use as a unit in our thought.

Language, therefore, makes thought easier and its accomplishment greater. After we have studied Cæsar for some years, the name comes to represent the epitome, the bird's-eye view of a great man. A similar thing is true of our study of other men and movements and things. Single words come to represent a multitude of experiences. Then these words become associated and organized in accordance with the principles of association discussed above, so that it comes about that the older we are, the more we come to think in words, and the more these words represent. The older we are, the more abstract our thinking becomes, the more do our words come to stand for meanings and attributes and laws that have come out of the organization of our experience.

It is evident that the accuracy of our thinking depends upon these words standing for the *truth*, depends upon whether we have organized our experience in accordance with facts. If our word "Cæsar" does not stand for the real Cæsar, then all our thinking in which Cæsar enters will be incorrect. If our word "justice" does not stand for the real justice, then all our thinking in which justice enters will be incorrect.

This discussion points to the tremendous importance of the organization of experience. Truth is the agreement of our thought with the thing, with reality. We must therefore help the young to see the world clearly and to organize what they see in accordance with the facts and with a view to future use. Then the units of this organized experience are to be tagged, labeled, by means of words, and these words or labels become the vehicles of thought, and the outcome of the thinking depends on the validity of the organization of our experience.

SUMMARY. Thinking is the passing of ideas in the mind; its basis is in the association of memory ideas. The basis of association is in original experience, ideas becoming bound together in memory as originally experienced. The factors of association are primacy, recency, frequency, intensity, and mental set or attitude. Reasoning is thinking to a purpose. We can be trained in reasoning by being taught to get vivid experience in the first place and in organizing this experience in helpful ways, having in mind future use.

CLASS EXERCISES

1.   A series of experiments should be performed to make clear to the students that the basis of the association of ideas is in *experience* and not in the nature of the ideas themselves.

a.   Let the students, starting with the same word, write down all the ideas that come to mind in one minute. The teacher should give the initial idea, as sky, hate, music, clock, table, or wind. The first ten ideas coming to each student might be written on the blackboard for study and comparison. Are any series alike? Is the tenth idea in one series the same as that in any other?

b.   For a study of the various factors of association, perform the following experiment: Let the teacher prepare a list of fifty words—nouns and adjectives, such as wood, murder, goodness, bad, death, water, love, angel. Read the words to the class and let each student write down the first idea that comes to mind in each case. After the list is finished, let each student try to find out what the determining factor was in each case, whether primacy, frequency, recency, vividness, or mental set. When the study is completed, the student's paper should contain three columns, the first column showing the stimulus words, the second showing the response words, the third showing the determining factors. The first column should be dictated and copied after the response words have been written.

c.   Study the data in (a) and (b), noting the variety of ideas that come to different students for the same stimulus word. It will be seen that they come from a great variety of experiences and from all parts of one's life from childhood to the present, showing that all our experiences are bound together and that we can go from one point to any other, directly or indirectly.

2.   Perform an experiment to determine how each member of the class thinks, *i.e.* in what kind of imagery. Let each plan a picnic in detail. How do they do it? Do they see it or hear it or seem to act it? Or does it happen in words merely?

3.   Think of the events of yesterday. How do they come to you? Do your images seem to be visual, auditory, motor, or verbal? Do you seem to have all kinds of imagery? Is one kind predominant?

4.   Test the class for speed of free association as described.. Repeat the experiment at least five times and rank the members of the class from the results.

5.   Similarly, test speed for controlled association as described and rank the members of the class.

6.   Compare the rankings in Nos. 4 and 5.

7.   The teacher can extend the controlled association tests by preparing lists that show different kinds of logical relations with one another, from genus to species, from species to genus, from

verb to object, from subject to verb, etc. Do the students maintain the same rank in the various types of experiments? Do the ranks in these tests correspond to the students' ranks in thinking in the school subjects?

8.   At least two series of experiments in reasoning should be performed, one to show the nature of reasoning and the other to show the ability of the members of the class.

a.   Put several problems to the class, similar to the following: What happens to a wet board laid out in the sunshine? Explain. Suppose corn is placed in three vessels, 1, 2, and 3. Number 1 is sealed up air tight and kept warm? Number 2 is kept open and warm? Number 3 is kept open and warm and moist. What happens in each case? Explain.

Condensed milk does not sour as long as the can remains unopened. After the can is opened, the milk sours if allowed to become warm; it does not sour if kept frozen. Why? Two bars of metal are riveted together. One bar is lead, the other iron. What happens when the bars are heated to 150 C? 500 C? 1000 C? 2000 C? Answer the following questions: Is it ever right to steal? To kill a person? To lie? Which are unwise and mistaken, Republicans or Democrats?

In the above, do all come to the same conclusion? Why? Were any unable to come to a conclusion at all on some questions? Why? Do the experiments make it clear that reasoning is dependent upon experience?

b.   Let the teacher prepare five problems in reasoning well within the experience of the class, and find the speed and accuracy of the students in solving them. Compare the results with those in the controlled association tests. Test the class with various kinds of mechanical puzzles.

9.   The students should study several people to ascertain how well those people have their experience organized. Is their

experience available? Can they come to the point immediately, or, are they hazy, uncertain, and impractical?

10.   It is claimed that we have two types of people, theoretical and practical. This is to some extent true. What is the explanation?

11.   From the point of view of No. 10, compare teachers and engineers.

12.   If anything will work in theory, will it work in practice?

13.   From what you have learned in the chapter and from the experiments, write a paper on training in reasoning.

14.   What are the main defects of the schools with reference to training children to think?

15.   Make a complete outline of the chapter.

REFERENCES FOR CLASS READING

- COLVIN and BAGLEY: *Human Behavior*, Chapters XVI and XVIII.

- DEWEY: *How We Think*, Parts I and III.

- MÜNSTERBERG: *Psychology, General and Applied*, Chapters VIII and XII; also pp. 192–195.

- PILLSBURY: *Essentials of Psychology*, Chapters VI and IX.

- PYLE: *The Outlines of Educational Psychology*, Chapter XV.

- TITCHENER: *A Beginner's Psychology*, Chapters V, VI, and X.

CHAPTER IX

INDIVIDUAL DIFFERENCES

Physical Differences. One never sees two people whose bodies are exactly alike. They differ in height or weight or color of the skin. They differ in the color of the hair or eyes, in the shape of the head, or in such details as size and shape of the ear, size and shape of the nose, chin, mouth, teeth, feet, hands, fingers, toes, nails, etc. The anatomist tells us that we differ internally just as we do externally. While the internal structure of one person has the same general plan as that of another, there being the same number of bones, muscles, organs, etc., there are always differences in detail. We are built on the same plan, *i.e.* we are made after a common type. We vary, above and below this type or central tendency.

Weight may be taken for illustration. If we should weigh the first thousand men we meet, we should find light men, heavy men, and men of medium weight. There would be few light men, few heavy men, but many men of medium weight. This fact is well shown in diagram by what is known as a curve of distribution or frequency surface, which is constructed as follows: Draw a base line A B, and on this line mark off equal distances to represent the various weights. At the left end put the number representing the lightest men and at the right the number representing the heaviest men; the other weights come in between in order. Then select a scale; we will say a millimeter in height above the base line represents one person of the weight represented on the base, and in drawing the upper part of the figure, A C B, we have but to measure up one millimeter for each person weighed, of the weight indicated below on the base.

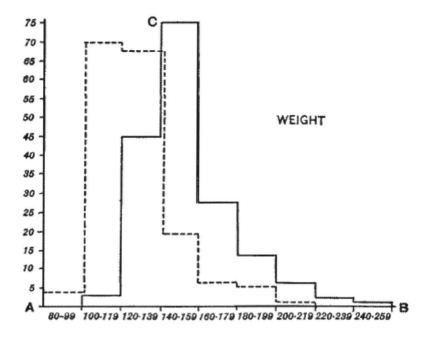

FIGURE V—FREQUENCY SURFACE—WEIGHT

The solid line represents men, the broken line, women.

A study of this frequency surface shows a tendency for people to be grouped about the central tendency or average. There are many people of average weight or nearly so, but few people who deviate widely from the average weight. If we measure people with reference to any other physical characteristic, or any mental characteristic, we get a similar result, we find them grouped about an average or central tendency.

Mental Differences. Just as we differ physically, so also we differ mentally, and in the various aspects of our behavior. The accompanying diagram (Free Association) shows the distribution of a large number of men and women with respect to the speed of their flow of ideas. When men and women are measured with respect to any mental function, a similar distribution is found.

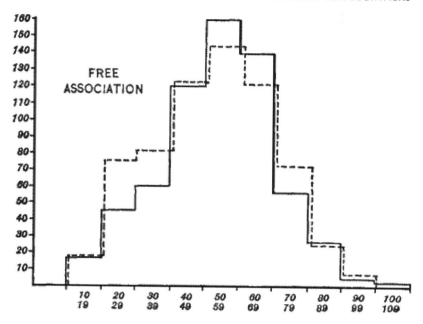

FIGURE VI—FREQUENCY SURFACE—FREE ASSOCIATION

Solid line, men; broken line, women. The numbers below the base represent the number of words written in the Free Association test, and the numbers at the left represent the number of people making the respective scores.

An interesting question is whether our mental differences have any relation or connection with one another. If one mental characteristic is of high order, are all the others of high order also? Does a good memory indicate a high order of attention, of association, of imagination, of learning capacity? Experiments show that mental characteristics have at least some degree of independence. But the rule is that they generally go together, a high order of ability in one mental function indicating a high order of ability in at least some others, and a low order of ability in one function indicating a low order in other functions.

However, it seems that abilities that are very much specialized, such as musical ability, artistic ability, etc., may exist in high order while other mental functions may be only mediocre. It is a common thing for a musical person to be of rather poor ability otherwise. To the extent that special abilities require specialized differences in the structure of brain, nervous system, or sense organ, they can exist in some degree of independence of other functions. Musical ability to some extent does require some such differences and may therefore be found either with a high or a low degree of ability in other characteristics.

It is doubtless true that at maturity the unequal power of mental functions in the same person may be partly due to the fact that one function has been exercised and others neglected. A person having very strong musical tendencies is likely to have such a great interest in music that he will think other activities are not worth while, and will consequently neglect these other activities. It will therefore turn out that at maturity the great differences in mental functions in such a person are in part due to exercise of one function and neglect of others. But there can be no doubt that in many cases there are large original, inherited differences, the individual being poor in one aspect of mind and good in others. Feeble-minded people are usually poor in all important aspects of mind. However, one sometimes finds a feeble-minded person having musical or artistic ability, and often such a person has a good rote memory, sometimes a good verbal memory. However, the so-called higher mental functions—logical memory, controlled association, and constructive imagination—are all poor in a feeble-minded person.

Each mental function may be looked upon as in some measure independent; each is found existing in people in varying degrees from zero ability up to what might be called genius ability. The frequency curves in Fig. VI show this. Take rote memory for example. Idiots are found with practically zero ability in rote memory. At the other extreme, we find mathematical prodigies who, after watching a long freight train pass and noting the numbers of the cars, can repeat correctly the number of each car. Rote memory abilities can be found representing every step between these two extremes. This principle of distribution holds true in the case of all mental functions. We find persons practically without them, and others possessing them in the highest order, but most people are grouped about the average ability.

Detecting Mental Differences. It has already been said that mind has many different aspects and that people differ with respect to these aspects. Now let us ask how we can measure the degree of development of these aspects or functions of mind. We measure them just as we measured muscular speed as described in the first chapter. Each mental function means ability to do something—to learn, to remember, to form images, to reason, etc. To measure these different capacities or functions we have but to require that the person under consideration *do* something, as learn, remember, etc., and measure how well and how fast he does it, just as we would measure how far he can jump, how fast he can run, etc.

In such measurements, the question of practice is always involved. If we measure running ability, we find that some are in practice while others are not. Those in practice can run at very nearly their ultimate capacity. Those who are not in practice can be trained to run much faster than they do. To get a true measure of running capacity, we should practice the persons to be measured till each runs up to the limit of his capacity, and then measure each one's speed. The same thing is true, to some extent, when we come to measure mental functions proper. However, the life that children live gives exercise to all fundamental functions of the mind, and unless some of the children tested have had experience which would tend to develop some mental functions in a special way, tests of the various aspects of learning capacity, memory, association, imagination, etc., are a fairly good measure of original, inherited tendencies.

Of course, it must be admitted that there are measurable differences in the influence of environment on children, and when these differences are extreme, no doubt the influence is shown in the development of the child's mind. A child reared in a home where all the influences favor its mental development, ought to show a measurable difference in such development when compared with a child reared in a home where all the influences are unfavorable. It is difficult to know to what extent this is true, for the hereditary and environmental influences are usually in harmony, the child of good hereditary stock having good environmental influences, and vice versa. When this is not the case, *i.e.* when a child of good stock is reared under poor environmental influences, or when a child of poor stock is reared under good influences, the results seem to show that the differences in environment have little effect on mental development, as far as the fundamental functions are concerned, except in the most extreme cases.

Each mental function is capable of some development. It can be brought up to the limit of its possibilities. But recent experiments indicate that such development is not very great in the case of the elementary, fundamental functions. Training, however, has a much greater effect on complex mental activities that involve several functions. Rote memory is rather simple; it cannot be much affected by training. The memory for ideas is more complex; it can be considerably affected by training. The original and fundamental functions of the mind depend upon the nature of the nervous system which is bequeathed to us by heredity. This cannot be much changed. However, training has considerable effect on the coördinations and combinations of mental functions. Therefore, the more complex the mental activities which we are testing, the more likely they are to have been affected by differences in experience and training.

If we should designate the logical memory capacity of one person by 10, and that of another by 15, by practice we might bring the first up to 15 and the second to 22 , but we could not equalize them. We could never make the memory of the one equal to that of the other. In an extreme case, we might find one child whose experience had been such that his logical memory was working up to the limit of its capacity, while the other had had little practice in logical memory and was therefore far below his real capacity. In such a case, a test would not show the native difference, it would show only the present difference in functioning capacity.

Fairly adequate tests for the most important mental functions have been worked out. A series of group tests with directions and norms follow. The members of the class can use these tests in studying the individual differences in other people. The teacher will find other tests in the author's *Examination of School Children*, and in Whipple's *Manual of Mental and Physical Tests*.

MENTAL TESTS

General Directions

The results of the mental tests in the school will be worse than useless unless the tests are given with the greatest care and scientific precision. Every test should be most carefully explained to the children so that they will know *exactly* what they are to do. The matter must be so presented to them that they will put forth *all possible* effort. They must take the tests seriously. Great care must be taken to see that there is no cheating. The work of each child should be his own work. In those tests in which time is an important element, the time must be *carefully kept*, with a stop watch if one is available. The papers should be distributed for the tests and turned face downward on the pupil's desk. The pupil, when all are ready to begin, should take the paper in his hand and at the signal "begin" turn it over and begin work, and when the signal "stop" is given, should quit work instantly and turn the paper over. Before the work begins, the necessary information should be placed on each paper. This information should be the pupil's name, age, grade, sex, and school. This should be on every paper. When the test is over the papers should be immediately collected.

Logical Memory

Object. The purpose of this test is to determine the pupil's facility in remembering and reproducing ideas. A pupil's standing in the test may serve as an indication of his ability to remember the subject matter of the school studies.

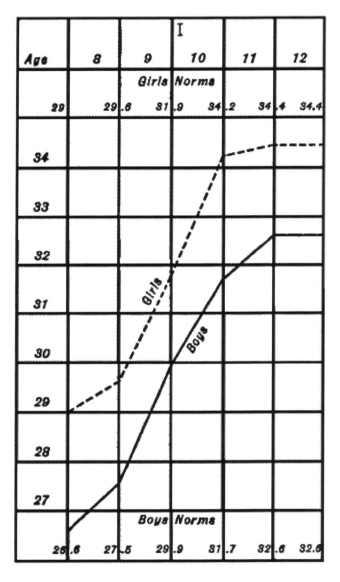

FIGURE VII—LOGICAL MEMORY—"WILLIE JONES"

Method. The procedure in this test is for the teacher to read slowly and distinctly the story to be reproduced. Immediately after the reading the pupils are to write down all of the story that they can recall. They must not begin to write till *after* the reading. Ten minutes should be allowed for the reproduction. This is ample time, and each pupil should be told to use the whole time in working on his reproduction. At the end of ten minutes, collect the papers. Care should be taken to see that each pupil does his own work, that there is no copying. Before reading the story, the teacher should give the following instructions:

I shall read to you a story entitled "Willie Jones and His Dog" (or "A Farmer's Son," or "A Costly Temper," as the case may be). After I have read the story you are to write down all you can remember of it. You are not to use the exact words that I read unless you wish. You are to use your own words. Try to recall as much as possible and write all you recall. Try to get all the details, not merely the main facts.

Material. For grades three, four, and five, use "Willie Jones and His Dog"; for grades six, seven, and eight, use "A Farmer's Son"; for the high school, use "A Costly Temper." The norms for the latter are based on eighth grade and high school pupils.

WILLIE JONES AND HIS DOG

Willie | Jones | was a little | boy | only | five years old. | He had a dog | whose name was Buster. | Buster was a large | dog | with long, | black, | curly | hair. | His fore | feet | and the tip | of his tail | were white. | One day | Willie's mother | sent him | to the store | which was only | a short | distance away. | Buster went with him, | following behind. | As Buster was turning | at the corner, | a car | struck him | and broke | one | hind | leg | and hurt | one | eye. | Willie was | very | sorry | and cried | a long | time. | Willie's father | came | and carried | the poor | dog | home. | The broken leg | got well | in five | weeks | but the eye | that was hurt | became blind. |

A FARMER'S SON

Will | was a farmer's | son | who attended school | in town. | His clothes | were poor and his boots | often smelled | of the farmyard | although he took great | care of them. | Since Will had not gone to school | as much | as his classmates, | he was often | at a disadvantage, | although his mind | was as good | as theirs,—| in fact, he was brighter | than most | of them. | James, | the wit | of the class, | never lost an opportunity | to ridicule | Will's mistakes, | his bright | red | hair, | and his patched | clothes. | Will | took the ridicule | in good part | and never | lost his temper. | One Saturday | as Will | was driving | his cows | to pasture, | he met James | teasing | a young | child, | a cripple. | Will's | indignation | was aroused | by the sight. | He asked | the bully | to stop, | but when he would not, | Will pounced | upon him | and gave him | a good | beating, | and he would not | let James go | until he promised | not to tease | the crippled | child | again. |

A COSTLY TEMPER

A man | named John | Murdock | had a servant | who worried him | much by his stupidity. | One day | when this servant was more | stupid | than usual, | the angry | master | of the house | threw a book | at his head. | The servant | ducked | and the book flew | out of the window. |

"Now go | and pick that book up!" | ordered the master. | The servant | started | to obey, | but a passerby | had saved him | the trouble, | and had walked off | with the book. | The scientist | thereupon | began to wonder | what book | he had thrown away, | and to his horror, | discovered | that it was a quaint | and rare | little | volume | of poems, | which he had purchased | in London | for fifty | dollars. |

But his troubles | were not over. | The weeks went by | and the man had almost | forgotten his loss, | when, strolling | into a secondhand | bookshop, | he saw, | to his great delight, | a copy of the book | he had lost. | He asked the price. |

"Well," | said the dealer, | reflectively, | "I guess we can let you have it | for forty | dollars. | It is a very | rare book, | and I am sure | that I could get seventy-five | dollars for it | by holding on a while." |

The man of science | pulled out his purse | and produced the money, | delighted at the opportunity of replacing | his lost | treasure. | When he reached home, | a card | dropped out | of the leaves. | The card was his own, | and further | examination | showed that he had bought back | his own property. |

"Forty dollars' | worth of temper," | exclaimed the man. | "I think I shall mend my ways." | His disposition | afterward | became so | good | that | the servant became worried, | thinking the man | must be ill. |

The Results. The material for the test is divided into units as indicated by the vertical lines. The pupil's written reproduction should be compared unit by unit with the story as printed, and given one credit for each unit adequately reproduced. The norms for the three tests are shown in the accompanying Figures VII, VIII, and IX. In these and all the graphs which follow, the actual ages are shown in the first horizontal column. The norms for girls appear in the second horizontal column, the norms for boys in the column at the bottom. By the *norm* for an age is meant the average performance of all the pupils of that age examined. Age ten applies to those pupils who have passed their tenth birthday and have not reached their eleventh birthday, and the other ages are to be similarly interpreted. The vertical lines in the graphs indicate birthdays and the scores written on these lines indicate ability at these exact ages. The column marked ten, for example, includes all the children that are over ten and not yet eleven. The graphs show the development from age to age. In general, it will be noticed, there is an improvement of memory with age, but in the high school, in the "Costly Temper" test, there is a decline. This may not indicate a real decline in ability to remember ideas, but a change in attitude. The high school pupil probably acquires a habit of remembering only significant facts. His memory is selective, while in the earlier ages, the memory may be more parrot-like, one idea being reproduced with about as much fidelity as another. This statement is made not as a *fact*, but as a *probable* explanation.

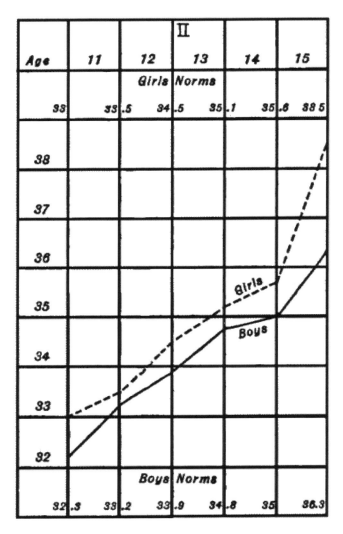

FIGURE VIII—LOGICAL MEMORY—"A FARMER'S SON"

Rote Memory

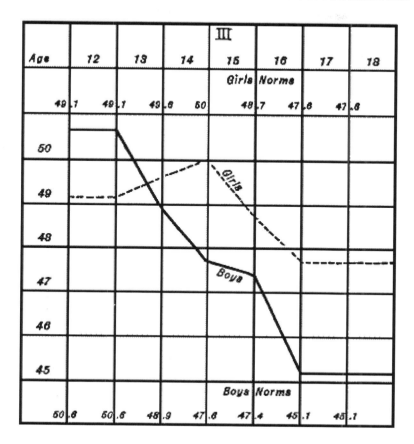

Age	12	13	14	15	16	17	18
				Girls	Norms		
	49.7	49.7	49.6	50	48.7	47.6	47.6

FIGURE IX—LOGICAL MEMORY—"A COSTLY TEMPER"

Object. The object of the rote memory tests is to determine the pupil's memory span for unrelated impressions—words that have no logical relations with one another. Much school work makes demands upon this ability. Therefore, the tests are of importance.

Method. There are two lists of words, *concrete* and *abstract*, with six groups in each list. The list of concrete words should be given first, then the abstract. The procedure is to pronounce the first group, *cat, tree, coat,* and then pause for the pupils to write these three words. Then pronounce the next group, *mule, bird, cart, glass,* and pause for the reproduction, and so on through the list.

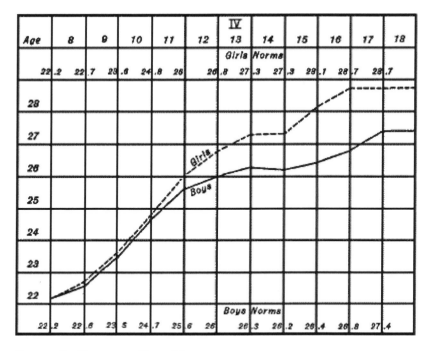

FIGURE X—CONCRETE ROTE MEMORY

Give the following instructions:

We wish to see how well you can remember words. I shall pronounce first a group of three words. *After* I have pronounced them, you are to write them down. I shall then pronounce a group of four words, then one of five words, and so continue with a longer group each time. You must pay very close attention for I shall pronounce a group but once. You are not required to write the words in their order, but just as you recall them.

Material. The words for the test are given in the following lists:

Concrete		Abstract	
1.	cat, tree, coat	1.	good, black, fast
2.	mule, bird, cart, glass	2.	clean, tall, round, hot

3.   star, horse, dress, fence, man

3.   long, wet, fierce, white, cold

4.   fish, sun, head, door, shoe, block

4.   deep, soft, quick, dark, great, dead

5.   train, mill, box, desk, oil, pup, bill

5.   sad, strong, hard, bright, fine, glad, plain

6.   floor, car, pipe, bridge, hand, dirt, cow, crank

6.   sharp, late, sour, wide, rough, thick, red, tight

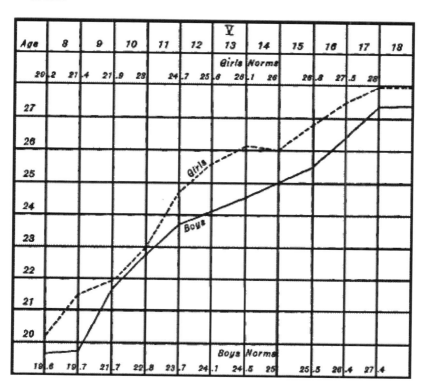

FIGURE XI—ABSTRACT ROTE MEMORY

Results. The papers are graded by determining the number of concrete words and the number of abstract words that are reproduced. No account is taken of whether the words are in the right position or not. A perfect score in each test would therefore be thirty-three. The norms are shown in Figures X and XI.

The Substitution Test

Object. This test determines one's ability to build up new associations. It is a test of quickness of learning.

Method. The substitution test-sheets are distributed to the pupils and turned face down on the desks. The teacher gives the following instructions:

We wish to see how fast you can learn. At the top of the sheet which has been distributed to you there is a key. In nine circles are written the nine digits and for each digit there is written a letter which is to be used instead of the digit. Below the key are two columns of numbers; each number contains five digits. In the five squares which follow the number you are to write the letters which correspond to the digits. Work as fast as you can and fill as many of the squares as you can without making mistakes. When I say "stop," quit work instantly and turn the paper over.

Before beginning the test the teacher should explain on the blackboard the exact nature of the test. This can be done by using other letters instead of those used in the key. Make sure that the pupils understand what they are to do. Allow *eight* minutes in grades three, four, and five, and *five* minutes above the fifth grade.

Material. For material, use the substitution test-sheets. This and the other test material can be obtained from the University of Missouri, Extension Division.

Results. In grading the work, count each square correctly filled in as one point, and reduce the score to speed per minute by dividing by eight in grades three, four, and five, and by five in the grades above.

The norms are shown in Figure XII.

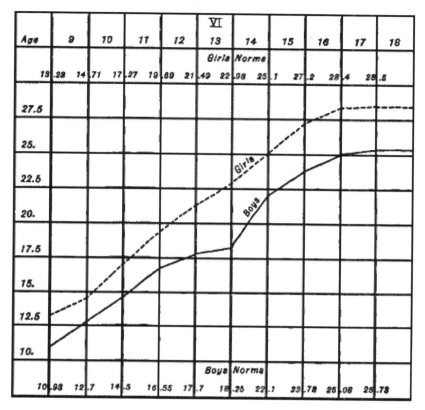

FIGURE XII—SUBSTITUTION TEST

Free Association

Object. This test determines the speed of the free flow of ideas. The result of the test is a criterion of the quickness of the flow of ideas when no restriction or limitation is put on this flow.

Method. The procedure in this test is to give the pupils a word, and tell them to write this word down and all the other words that come into their minds. Make it clear to them that they are to write whatever word comes to mind, whether it has any relation to the word that is given them or not. Start them with the word "cloud." Give the following instructions:

I wish to see how many words you can think of and write down in three minutes. I shall name a word, you may write it down and then all the other words that come into your minds. Do not write sentences, merely the words that come into your minds. Work as fast as you can.

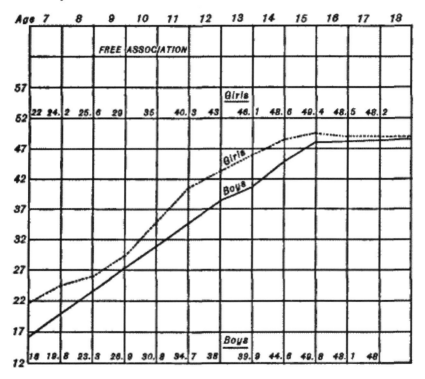

FIGURE XIII—FREE ASSOCIATION TEST

Results. Score the work by counting the number of words that have been written. The norms are shown in Figure XIII.

Opposites

Object. This is a test of controlled association. It tests one aspect of the association of ideas. All thinking is a matter of association of ideas. Reasoning is controlled association. The test may therefore be taken as a measure of speed in reasoning.

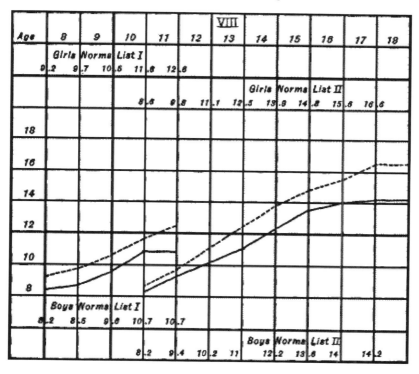

FIGURE XIV—OPPOSITES TEST—LISTS I AND II

Method. Distribute the lists of opposites to the pupils and turn them face down on the desks. Use List One in grades three, four, and five, and List Two in grades above. Allow two minutes in grades three, four, and five and one minute in grades above. Give the following instructions:

On the sheets that have been distributed to you are fifty words. After each word you are to write a word that has the opposite meaning. For example, if one word were "far," you could write "near." Work as fast as you can, and when I say "stop" quit work instantly and turn your paper over.

Results. The score is the number of opposites correctly written. The norms are shown in Figure XIV.

OPPOSITES—LIST NO. 1		OPPOSITES—LIST NO. 2	
1.	good	1.	strong
2.	big	2.	deep
3.	rich	3.	lazy
4.	out	4.	seldom
5.	sick	5.	thin
6.	hot	6.	soft
7.	long	7.	many
8.	wet	8.	valuable
9.	yes	9.	gloomy
10.	high	10.	rude
11.	hard	11.	dark
12.	sweet	12.	rough
13.	clean	13.	pretty
14.	sharp	14.	high
15.	fast	15.	foolish
16.	black	16.	present

17.	old	17.	glad
18.	up	18.	strange
19.	thick	19.	wrong
20.	quick	20.	quickly
21.	pretty	21.	black
22.	heavy	22.	good
23.	late	23.	fast
24.	wrong	24.	clean
25.	smooth	25.	tall
26.	strong	26.	hot
27.	dark	27.	long
28.	dead	28.	wet
29.	wide	29.	fierce
30.	empty	30.	great
31.	above	31.	dead
32.	north	32.	cloudy
33.	laugh	33.	hard
34.	man	34.	bright
35.	before	35.	fine
36.	winter	36.	plain
37.	ripe	37.	sharp

38.	night	38.	late
39.	open	39.	sour
40.	first	40.	wide
41.	over	41.	drunk
42.	love	42.	tight
43.	come	43.	empty
44.	east	44.	sick
45.	top	45.	friend
46.	wise	46.	above
47.	front	47.	loud
48.	girl	48.	war
49.	sad	49.	in
50.	fat	50.	yes

The Word-Building Test

Object. This is a test of a certain type of inventiveness, namely linguistic invention. Specifically, it tests the pupil's ability to construct words using certain prescribed letters.

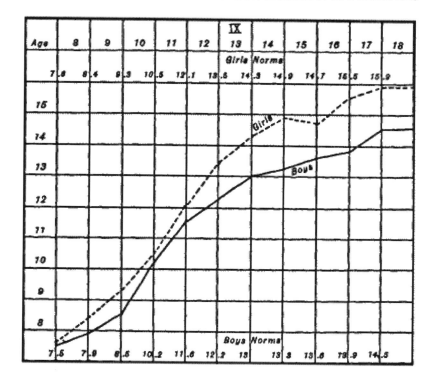

FIGURE XV—WORD-BUILDING TEST

Method. The pupils are given the letters, *a, e, o, m, n, r,* and told to make as many words as possible using only these letters. Give the following instructions:

I wish to see how many words you can make in five minutes, using only the letters which I give you. The words must be real English words. You must use only the letters which I give you and must not use the same letter more than once in the same word. You do not, of course, have to use all the letters in the same word. A word may contain one or more letters up to six.

Material. The pupils need only sheets of blank paper.

Results. The score is the number of words that do not violate the rules of the test as given in the instructions. The norms are shown in Figure XV.

The Completion Test

Object. This is, to some extent, a test of reasoning capacity. Of course, it is only one particular aspect of reasoning. The pupil is given a story that has certain words omitted. He must read the story, see what it is trying to say, and determine what words, put into the blanks, will make the correct sense. The meaning of the word written in a particular blank must not only make the sentence read sensibly but must fit into the story *as a whole*. Filling in the blanks in this way demands considerable thought.

Method. Distribute the test-sheets and turn them face down on the desks. Allow ten minutes in all the tests. Give the following instructions:

On the sheets which have been distributed is printed a story which has certain words omitted. You are to put in the blanks the words that are omitted. The words which you write in must give the proper meaning so that the story reads correctly. Each word filled in must not only give the proper meaning to the sentence but to the story as a whole.

Material. Use the completion test-sheets, "Joe and the Fourth of July," for grades three, four, and five; "The Trout" for grades, six, seven, and eight; and "Dr. Goldsmith's Medicine" for the high school.

Results. In scoring the papers, allow one credit for each blank correctly filled. The norms are shown in Figures XVI, XVII, and XVIII. It will be noticed that the boys excel in the "Trout" story. This is doubtless because the story is better suited to them on the ground of their experience and interest.

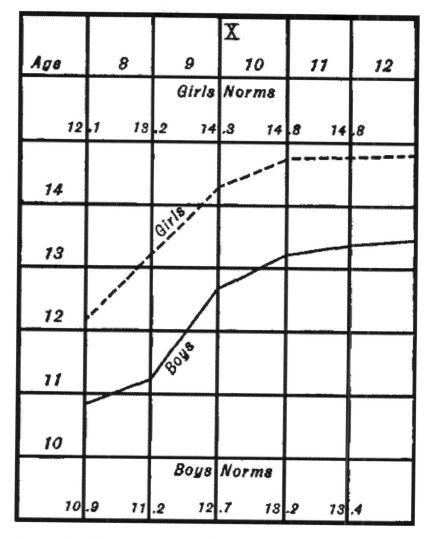

Age	8	9	**X** 10	11	12
			Girls Norms		
	12.1	13.2	14.3	14.8	14.8
14					
13					
12					
11					
10					
			Boys Norms		
	10.9	11.2	12.7	13.2	13.4

FIGURE XVI—COMPLETION TEST—"JOE AND THE FOURTH OF JULY"

JOE AND THE FOURTH OF JULY

Joe *ran* errands for *his* mother and *took* care of the *baby* until by the Fourth of July his penny *grew* to be a dime. The day before the

Fourth, he *went* down town all by *himself* to get his fire *works*. There were so *many* kinds he hardly knew which to *buy*. The clerk knew that it takes a *long* time to decide, for he had been a *boy* himself not very *long* ago. So he helped Joe to *select* the very best kinds. "When are you going to *fire* them off?" asked the clerk. "I will fire *them* very *early* to-morrow," said the boy. So that night Joe set the *alarm* clock, and the next *morning* got up *early* to fire his firecrackers.

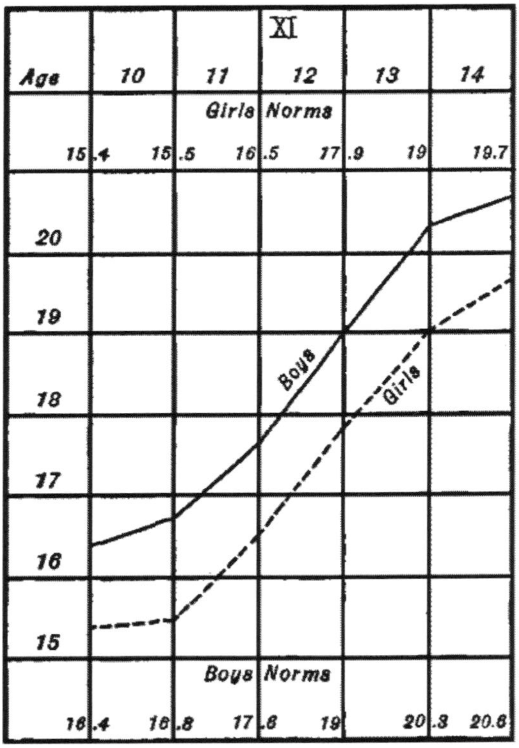

FIGURE XVII—COMPLETION TEST—"THE TROUT"

THE TROUT

The trout is a fine fish. Once a big trout *lived* in a pool *close* by a spring. He used to *stay* under the bank with *only* his head showing. His wide-open *eyes* shone like jewels. I tried to *catch* him. I would *creep* up to the *edge* of the pool *where* I could see his *bright* eyes looking up.

I *caught* a grasshopper and *threw* it over *to* him. Then there was a *splash* in the water and the grasshopper *was gone.* I *did* this *two* or three times. Each time I *saw* the rush and splash and saw the bait had been *taken.*

So I put the same bait on my *hook* and *threw* it over into the *water.* But *all* was silent. The fish was an *old* one and had *grown* very wise. I did this *day* after day with the same luck. The trout *knew* there was a *hook* hidden in the bait.

DOCTOR GOLDSMITH'S MEDICINE

This *is* a story of good medicine. Most medicine is *bad* to *take,* but this was so good *that* the sick man *wished* for more.

One day a poor woman *went* to Doctor Goldsmith and *asked* him to *go* to see her *sick* husband. "He *is* very sick," she said, "and I *can* not *get* him to eat anything."

So Doctor Goldsmith *went* to *see* him. The doctor *saw* at once that the *reason* why the man *could* not eat was *because* he was *so* poor that he had *not* been *able* to buy good food.

Then he *said* to the woman, "*Come* to my house this evening and I will *give you* some *medicine* for your *husband.*"

The woman *went* in the evening and the *doctor* gave *her* a small paper box tied *up* tight. "*It* is very heavy," she said. "May I *see* what it looks *like?*" "*No,*" said the doctor, "*wait* until you get *home.*" When she *got* home, and she and *her* husbandopened the box so that he *could* take the first *dose* of medicine,—what do you think they *saw?* The box was *filled* with silver *money. This* was the *good* doctor's medicine.

Importance of Mental Differences. (1) *In school work.* One of the important results that come from a knowledge of the mental differences in children is that we are able to classify them better. When a child enters school he should be allowed to proceed through the course as fast as his development warrants. Some children can do an eight-year course in six years; others require ten years; still others can never do it. The great majority, of course, can do it in eight years.

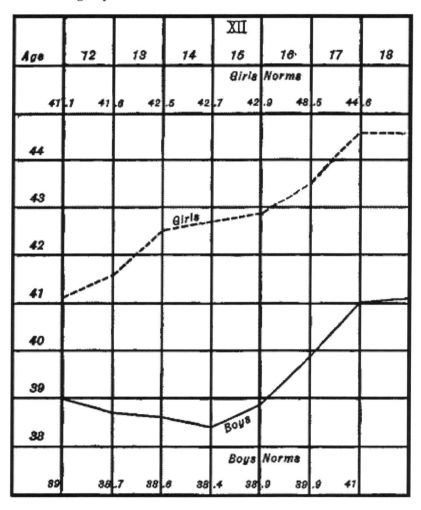

FIGURE XVIII—COMPLETION TEST—"DR. GOLDSMITH'S MEDICINE"

Norms for adults, as obtained from university students, are:

TEST	MEN	WOMEN
Substitution Test	29.1	32.2
Rote Memory, Concrete	28.5	28.6
Rote Memory, Abstract	28.4	27.9
Free Association	51.5	49.3
Completion, *Dr. Goldsmith's Medicine*	48.1	49.0
Word Building	20.5	20.1
Logical Memory, *Costly Temper*	64.0	69.6

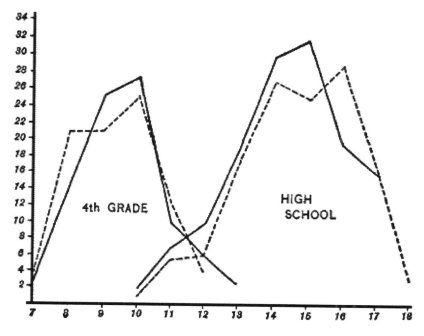

FIGURE XIX—FREQUENCY SURFACES—COMPARING FOURTH GRADE WITH HIGH SCHOOL

The numbers along the base represent mental age; those at the left, the number of pupils of the respective ages.

It may be thought that a child's success in school branches is a sufficient measure of his ability and that no special mental measurements are needed. This is a mistake. Many factors contribute to success in school work. Ability is only one of these factors, and should be specially and independently determined by suitable tests. Children may fail in school branches because of being poorly started or started at the wrong time, because of poor teaching, sickness, moving from one school to another, etc. On the other hand, children of poor ability may succeed at school because of much help at home. Therefore special mental tests will help in determining to what extent original mental ability is a factor in the success or failure of the different pupils.

As far as possible, the children of the same grade should have about the same ability; but such is seldom the case. In a recent psychological study of a school system, the author found wide differences in ability in the same grade. The distribution of abilities found in the fourth grade and in the high school are shown in Figure XIX. It will be seen that in the fourth grade pupils are found with ability equal to that of some in the high school. Of course to some extent such a condition is unavoidable, for a pupil must establish certain habits and acquire certain knowledge before passing from one grade to another. However, much of the wide variation in ability now found in the same grade of a school could be avoided if the teacher had accurate knowledge of the pupils' abilities. When a teacher learns that a child who is doing poorly in school really has ability, she is often able to get from that pupil the work of which he is capable. It has been demonstrated by experience that accurate measures of children's abilities are a great help in gradation and classification.

A knowledge of mental differences is also an aid in the actual teaching of the children. The instance mentioned at the close of the last paragraph is an example. A knowledge of the differences among the mental functions of the same pupil is especially helpful. It has been pointed out that the different mental functions in the same pupil are sometimes unequally developed. Sometimes considerable differences exist in the same pupil with respect to learning capacity, the different aspects of memory, association, imagination, and attention. When a teacher knows of these differences, she can better direct the work of the pupils.

For example, if a pupil have a very poor memory, the teacher can help him by aiding him to secure the advantage that comes from close and concentrated attention, frequent repetitions, logical organization, etc. On the other hand, she can help the brilliant student by preventing him from being satisfied with hastily secured, superficial knowledge, and by encouraging him to make proper use of his unusual powers in going deeper and more extensively into the school subjects than is possible for the ordinary student. In many ways a teacher can be helpful to her pupils if she has an accurate knowledge of their mental abilities.

(2) *In life occupations*. Extreme variations in ability should certainly be considered in choosing one's life work. Only persons of the highest ability should go into science, law, medicine, or teaching. Many occupations demand special kinds of ability, special types of reaction, of attention, imagination, etc. For example, the operation of a telephone exchange demands a person of quick and steady reaction. The work of a motorman on a street car demands a person having the broad type of attention, the type of attention that enables one to keep in mind many details at the same time. Scientific work demands the type of concentrated attention. As far as it is possible, occupations demanding special types of ability should be filled by people possessing these abilities. It is best for all concerned if each person is doing what he can do best. It is true that many occupations do not call for special types of ability. And therefore, as far as ability is concerned, a person could do as well in

one of these occupations as in another. The time will sometime come when we shall know the special abilities demanded by the different occupations and professions, and by suitable tests shall be able to determine what people possess the required qualifications.

The schools should always be on the lookout for unusual ability. Children that are far superior to others of the same age should be allowed to advance as fast as their superior ability makes possible, and should be held up to a high order of work. Such superior people should be, as far as possible, in the same classes, so that they can the more easily be given the kind and amount of work that they need. The schools should find the children of unusual special ability, such as ability in drawing, painting, singing, playing musical instruments, mechanical invention, etc. Some provision should be made for the proper development and training of these unusual abilities. Society cannot afford to lose any spark of genius wherever found. Moreover, the individual will be happier if developed and trained along the line of his special ability.

Subnormal Children. A small percentage of children are of such low mentality that they cannot do the ordinary school work. As soon as such children can be picked out with certainty, they should be taken out of the regular classes and put into special classes. It is a mistake to try to get them to do the regular school work. They cannot do it, and they only waste the teacher's time and usually give her much trouble. Besides, they waste their own time; for while they cannot do the ordinary school work, they can do other things, perhaps work of a manual nature. The education of such people should, therefore, be in the direction of simple manual occupations.

For detecting such children, in addition to the tests given above, elaborate tests for individual examination have been devised. The most widely used is a series known as the Binet-Simon tests. A special group of tests is provided for the children of each age. If a child can pass the tests for his age, he is considered normal. If he can pass only the tests three years or more below his age, he is usually considered subnormal. But a child's fate should not depend solely upon any number or any kind of tests. We should always give the child a trial and see what he is able to achieve. This trial should cover as many months or years as are necessary to determine beyond doubt the child's mental status.

SUMMARY. Just as we differ in the various aspects of body, so also we differ in the various aspects of mind. These differences can be measured by tests. A knowledge of these differences should aid us in grading, classifying, and teaching children, as well as in the selection of occupation and professions for them. Mental traits have some degree of independence; as a result a high degree of one trait may be found with low degree of some others.

CLASS EXERCISES

1.   Many of the tests and experiments already described should have shown many of the individual differences of the members of the class. The teacher will find in the author's *Examination of School Children* a series of group tests with norms which can be used for a further study of individual differences.

2.   The tapping experiment described in the first chapter can now be repeated and the results taken as a measure of reaction time.

3.   You should now have available the records of all the tests and experiments so far given that show individual differences. Make out a table showing the rank of each student in the various tests. Compute the average rank of each student for all the tests. This average rank may be taken as a measure of the intelligence of the students, as far as such can be determined by the tests used. Correlate this ranking with standing in the high school classes. It will give a positive correlation, not perfect, however. Why not? If your measures of intelligence were absolutely correct, you still would not get a perfect correlation with high school standing. Why not?

4.   If you had a correct measure of intelligence of 100 mature people in your city, selected at random, would this measure give you an exact measure of their success in life? Give the reason for your answer.

5.   Of all the tests and experiments previously described in this book, which gives the best indication of success in high school?

6.   If the class in psychology is a large one, a graph should be prepared showing the distribution of abilities in the class. For this purpose, you will have to use the absolute measures instead of ranks. Find the average for each test used. Make these averages all the same by multiplying the low ones and dividing the high ones. Then all the grades of each student can be added. This will give each test the same weight in the average. The use of a slide rule will make this transference to a new average very easy. A more accurate method for this computation is described in the author's *Examination of School Children*, p. 65.

The students should make a study of individual differences and the distribution of ability in some grade below the high school. The tests described in this chapter can be used for that purpose.

7.   Is it a good thing for high school students to find out how they compare with others in their various mental functions? If you have poor ability, is it a good thing for you to find it out? If the teacher and students think best, the results of all the various tests need not be made known except to the persons concerned. The data can be used in the various computations without the students' knowing whose measures they are.

8.   To what extent is ability a factor in life? You find people of only ordinary ability succeeding and brilliant people failing. Why is this?

9.   None of the tests so far used measures ideals or perseverance and persistence. These are important factors in life, and there is no very adequate measure for any of them. The

students might plan some experiments to test physical and mental persistence and endurance. The tapping experiment, for example, might be continued for an hour and the records kept for each minute. Then from these records a graph could be plotted showing the course of efficiency for the hour. Mental adding or mul tiplying might be kept up continuously for several hours and the results studied as above.

10.   We have said that ideals and persistence are important factors in life. Are they inherited or acquired?

11.   Do you find it to be the rule or the exception for a person standing high in one mental function to stand high in the others also?

12.   Make a complete outline of the chapter.

REFERENCES FOR CLASS READING

- MÜNSTERBERG: *Psychology, General and Applied.* Chapter XVI.

- PYLE: *The Examination of School Children.*

- PYLE: *The Outlines of Educational Psychology.* Chapter XVII.

- TITCHENER: *A Beginner's Psychology,* pp. 309–311.

CHAPTER X

APPLIED PSYCHOLOGY

The General Field. Psychology has now reached that stage in its development where it can be of use to humanity. It can be of use in those fields which demand a knowledge of human nature. As indicated in the first chapter, these fields are education, medicine, law, business, and industry. We may add another which has been called "culture." We cannot say that psychology is able yet to be of very great service except to education, law, and medicine. It has been of less service to the field of business and industry, but in the future, its contribution here will be as great as in the other fields. While the service of psychology in the various fields is not yet great, what it will eventually be able to do is very clear. It is the purpose of this chapter to indicate briefly, the nature and possibilities of this psychological service.

Education. Throughout the preceding chapters, we have emphasized the educational importance of the facts discussed. There is little left to say here except to summarize the main facts. Since education is a matter of making a child over into what he ought to be, the science of education demands a knowledge of the original nature of children. This means that one must know the nature of instincts, their relations to one another, their order of development, and the possibilities of their being changed, modified, developed, suppressed. It means that one must know the nature of the child's mind in all its various functions, the development and significance of these functions,—memory, association, imagination, and attention. The science especially demands that we understand the principles of habit-formation, the laws of economical learning, and the laws of memory.

This psychological knowledge must form the ground-work in the education of teachers for their profession. In addition to this general preparation of the teacher, psychology will render the

189

schools a great service through the psycho-clinicist, who will be a psychological expert working under the superintendents of our school systems. His duty will be to supervise the work of mental testing, the work of diagnosis for feeble-mindedness and selection of the subnormal children, the teaching of such children. He will give advice in all cases which demand expert psychological knowledge.

Medicine. In the first place, there is a department of medicine which deals with nervous diseases, such as insanity, double personality, severe nervous shock, hallucination, etc. This entire aspect of medicine is wholly psychological. But psychology can be of service to the general practitioner both in the diagnosis and treatment of disease. A thorough psychological knowledge of human nature will assist a physician in diagnosis. Often the best way to find out what ails a patient's body is through the patient's mind, and the doctor must know how to get the truth from the patient's mind even in those cases in which the patient is actually trying to conceal the truth. A profound practical knowledge of human nature is neces sary,—a knowledge which can be obtained only by long and careful technical study as well as practice and experience.

Psychology can be of service in the treatment of disease. The physician must understand the peculiar mental characteristics of his patient in order to know how to deal with him. In some cases, hypnotism is a valuable aid in treatment, and in many cases, ordinary normal suggestion can be of considerable service. The state of mind of a sick person has much to do with his recovery. The physician must know this and must know how to induce the desired state of mind. Indeed, a patient's trouble is often imaginary, exists in the mind only; in such cases, the treatment should be wholly mental, *i.e.* through suggestion. Of course, the best physicians know these facts and make use of them in their practice, but preparation for this aspect of their work should be a regular part of their medical education. They should not be left to learn these facts from their practice as best they may, any more than they should be expected to learn their physiology and anatomy in this way.

Law. The service of psychology to law can be very great, but owing to the necessary conservatism of the courts, it will be a long time before they will make much use of psychological knowledge. Perhaps the greatest service will be in determining the credibility of evidence. Psychology can now give the general principles in this matter. Witnesses go on the stand and swear to all sorts of things as to what they heard and saw and did, often months and even years previously. The expert clinical psychologist can tell the court the probability of such evidence being true. Experiments have shown that there is a large per centage of error in such evidence. The additional value that comes from the oath has been measured. The oath increases the liability of truth only a small percentage.

Experiments have also shown that one's feeling of certainty is no guarantee of truth. Sometimes the point we feel surest about is the one farthest from the truth. In fact, feeling sure of a thing is no guarantee of truth.

In a particular case in court, the psychologist can determine the reliability of the evidence of a particular witness and enable the judge and the jury to put the proper value on such witness's testimony. For example, a witness may swear to a certain point involving the estimation of time and distance. The psychologist can measure the witness's accuracy in such estimates, often showing that what the witness claims to be able to do is an impossibility. A case may hinge on whether an interval of time was ten minutes or twelve minutes, or whether a distance was three hundred or four hundred feet. A witness may swear positively to one or both of these points. The psychologist can show the court the limitations of the witness in making such estimates.

Psychology can be of service in the examination of the criminal himself. Through association tests and in other ways, the guilt or innocence of the prisoner can often be determined, and his intellectual status can also be determined. The prisoner may be insane, or feeble-minded, or have some other peculiar mental disorder. Such matters fall within the realm of psychology. After a prisoner has been found guilty, the court should have the advice of the clinical psychologist in deciding what should be done with him.

It should be added that the court and not the attorneys should make use of the psychologist. Whenever a psychologist can be of service in a case in court, the judge should summon such assistance, just as he should if expert chemical, physical, physiological, or anatomical knowledge should be desired.

A knowledge of human nature can be of much service to society in the prevention of crime. This will come about from a better knowledge of the psychological principles of habit-formation and moral training, through a better knowledge of how to control human nature. A large percentage of all crime, perhaps as much as forty per cent, is committed by feeble-minded people. Now, if we can detect these people early, and give them the simple manual education which they are capable of receiving, we can keep them out of a life of crime.

Studies of criminals in reform schools show that the history of many cases is as follows: The person, being of low mentality, could not get on well at school and therefore came to dislike school, and consequently became a truant. Truancy led to crime. Crime sent the person to the court, and the court sent the person to the state reformatory.

The great duty of the state is the prevention of crime. Usually little can be done in the way of saving a mature criminal. We must save the children before they become criminals, save them by proper treatment. Society owes it to every child to do the right thing for him, the right thing, whether the child is an idiot or a genius. Merely from the standpoint of economy, it would be an immense saving to the state if it would prevent crime by the proper treatment of every child.

Business. The contribution of psychology in this field, so far, is in the psychology of advertising and salesmanship, both having to do chiefly with the selling of goods. Students of the psychology of advertising have, by experiment, determined many principles that govern people when reading newspapers and magazines, principles having to do with size and kind of type, arrangement and form, the wording of an advertisement, etc. The object of an advertisement is to get the reader interested in the article advertised. The first thing is to get him to *read* the advertisement. Here, various principles of attention are involved. The next thing is to have the *matter* of the advertisement of such a nature that it creates interest and remains in memory, so that when the reader buys an article of that type he buys the particular kind mentioned in the advertisement.

In salesmanship, many subtle psychological principles are involved. The problem of the salesman is to get the attention of the customer, and then to make him *want* to buy his goods. To do this with the greatest success demands a profound knowledge of human nature. Other things being equal, that man can most influence people who has the widest knowledge of the nature of people, and of the factors that affect this nature. The successful salesman must understand human feelings and emotions, especially sympathy; also the laws of attention and memory, and the power of suggestion. A mastery of the important principles requires years of study, and a successful application of them requires just as many years of practice.

The last paragraph leads us to a consideration of the general problem of influencing men. In all occu pations and professions, one needs to know how to influence other men. We have already discussed the matter of influencing people to buy goods. People who employ labor need to know how to get laborers to do more and better work, how to make them loyal and happy. The minister needs to know how to induce the members of his congregation to do right. The statesman needs to know how to win his hearers and convince them of the justice and wisdom of his cause. Whatever our calling, there is scarcely a day when we could not do better if we knew more fully how to influence people.

Industry. The service of psychology here is four-fold: (1) Finding what men are fitted for. (2) Finding what kinds of abilities are demanded by the various trades and occupations. (3) Helping the worker to understand the psychological aspects of his work. (4) Getting the best work out of the laborer.

Finding what men are fitted for. In the preceding chapter, we discussed the individual variations of men. Some people are better fitted physically and mentally for certain types of work than they are for other types of work. The determination of what an individual is fitted for and what he is not fitted for is the business of psychology. In some cases, the verdict of psychology can be very specific; in others, it can be only general. Much misery and unhappiness come to people from trying to do what they are not fitted by nature to do. There are many professions and occupations which people should not enter unless they possess high general ability. Now, psychology is able to measure general ability. There are many other occupations and professions which people should not enter unless they possess some special ability. Music, art, and mechanics may be mentioned as examples of occupations and professions demanding specific kinds of ability. In industrial work, many aspects demand very special abilities, as quick reaction, quick perception, fine discrimination, calmness and self-control, ingenuity, quick adaptation to new situations. Psychology can aid in picking out the people who possess the required abilities.

The different abilities demanded. It is the business of psychology to make a careful analysis of the specific abilities required in all the various works of life. There are hundreds of occupations and often much differentiation of work within an occupation. It is for the psychologist of the future to make this analysis and to classify the occupations with reference to the kinds of abilities demanded. Of course, many of them will be found to require the same kind of ability, but just as surely, many will be found to require very special abilities. It is a great social waste to have people trying to fill such positions unless they possess the specific abilities required.

It should be the work of the high school and college to explain the possibilities, and the demands in the way of ability, of the various occupations of the locality. By possibilities and demands are meant the kinds of abilities required and the rewards that can be expected, the kind of life which the different fields offer. It is the further duty of the high school and college to find out, as far as possible, the specific abilities of the students. With this knowledge before them, the students should choose their careers, and then make specific preparation for them. The schools ought to work in close coöperation with the industries, the student working for a part of the day in school and a part in the industries. This would help much in leading the student to understand the industries and in ascertaining his own abilities and interests.

The psychological aspects of one's work. All occupations have a psychological aspect. They involve some trick of attention, of association, of memory. Certain things must be looked for, certain habits must be formed, certain movements must be automatized. Workmen should be helped to master these psychological problems, to find the most convenient ways of doing their work. Workmen often do their work in the most uneconomical ways, having learned their methods through imitation, and never inquiring whether there is a more economical way.

Securing efficiency. Securing efficiency is a matter of influencing men, a matter which we have already discussed. Securing efficiency is quite a different matter from that treated in the preceding paragraph. A workman may have a complete knowledge of his work and be skilled in its performance, and still be a poor workman, because he does not have the right attitude toward his employer or toward his work. The employer must therefore meet the problem of making his men like their work and be loyal to their employer. The laborer must be happy and contented if he is to do good work. Moreover, there is *no use in working*, or in living either, if one cannot be happy and contented.

We have briefly indicated the possibilities of psychology in the various occupations and professions. There is a further application that has no reference to the practical needs of life, but to enjoyment. A psychological knowledge of human nature adds a new interest to all our social experience. The ability to understand the actions and feelings of men puts new meaning into the world. The ability to understand oneself, to analyze one's actions, motives, feelings, and thoughts, makes life more worth living. A knowledge of the sensations and sense organs adds much pleasure to life in addition to its having great practical value. Briefly, a psychological knowledge of human nature adds much to the richness of life. It gives one the analytical attitude. Experiences that to others are wholes, to the psychologist fall apart into their elements. Such knowledge leads us to analyze and see clearly what otherwise we do not understand and see only darkly or not at all. Literature and art, and all other creations and products of man take on a wholly new interest to the psychologist.

SUMMARY. Psychology is of service to education in ascertaining the nature of the child and the laws of learning; to law, in determining the reliability of evidence and in the prevention of crime; to medicine, in the work of diagnosis and treatment; to business, in advertising and salesmanship; to the industries, in finding the man for the place and the place for the man; to everybody, in giving a keener insight into, and understanding of, human nature.

CLASS EXERCISES

1.   Visit a court room when a trial is in progress. Note wherein psychology could be of service to the jury, to the judge, and to the attorneys.

2.   To test the reliability of evidence, proceed as follows: Take a large picture, preferably one in color and having many details; hold it before the class in a good light where all can see it. Let them look at it for ten or fifteen seconds, the time depending on the complexity of the picture. The students should then write down what they saw in the picture, underscoring all the points to which

they would be willing to make oath. Then the students should answer a list of questions prepared by the teacher, on various points in the picture. Some of these questions should be suggestive, such as, "What color is the dog?" supposing no dog to be in the picture. The papers giving the first written description should be graded on the number of items reported and on their accuracy. The answers to the questions should be graded on their accuracy. How do girls compare with boys in the various aspects of the report? What is the accuracy of the underlined points?

3.   Let the teacher, with the help of two or three students, perform before the class some act or series of acts, with some conversation, and then have the students who have witnessed the performance write an account of it, as in No. 2.

4.   Divide the class into two groups. Select one person from each to look at a picture as in No. 1. These two people are then to write a complete account of the picture. This account is then read to another person in the same group, who then writes from memory his account and reads to another. This is to be continued till all have heard an account and written their own. You will then have two series of accounts of the same picture proceeding from two sources. It will be well for the two who look at the picture to be of very different types, let us say, one imaginative, the other matter-of-fact.

Do all the papers of one series have some characteristics that enable you to determine from which group they come? What conclusions and inferences do you draw from the experiment?

5.   Does the feeling of certainty make a thing true? See how many cases you can find in a week, of persons feeling sure a statement is true, when it is really false.

6.   In the following way, try to find out something which a person is trying to conceal. Prepare a list of words, inserting now and then words which have some reference to the vital point. Read the words one by one to the person and have him speak the first

word suggested by those read. Note the time taken for the responses. A longer reaction time usually follows the incriminating words, and the subject is thrown into a visible confusion.

7.   Talk to successful physicians and find out what use they make of suggestion and other psychological principles.

8.   Spend several hours visiting different grades below the high school. In how many ways could the teachers improve their work by following psychological principles?

9.   Could the qualities of a good teacher—native and acquired— be measured by tests and experiments?

10.   Visit factories where men do skillful work and try to learn by observation what types of mind and body are required by the different kinds of work.

11.   Does the occupation which you have chosen for life demand any specific abilities? If so, do you possess them in a high degree?

12.   Could parents better train their children if they made use of psychological principles?

13.   In how many ways will the facts learned in this course be of economic use to you in your life? In what ways will they make life more pleasurable?